THE PURPLE RIVER

Rick Glaze

ALSO BY RICK GLAZE

Books

Eight Pieces of Eight

Spanish Pieces of Eight

Ralph & Murray

Jackass, Short Story Collection

The Purple River

Music CDs

Anegada Caribbean Breeze

Silicon Cowboy

Writer's Path Blog

PREMIUM READER CLUB

Join my Premium Reader Club and be part of the excitement. I've enjoyed sailing and outdoor adventure for a long time and you can escape with me on these adventures by clicking below.

Get free books, free behind the scenes photos, original songs written for the books and more. Members are always first to hear about new offerings and publications. To join click on *Rick's Guide to the Virgin Islands* at:

https://www.RickGlaze.com

ScreenShot Publishers

Nashville, Tennessee

Ricksbooks@rickglaze.com

Second Edition

Cover Design: GologoNow

Editor: Mike Robinson

Formatting: Polgarus Studio

ISBN: 978-1-7372951-1-2 (paperback)

ISBN: 978-1-7372951-0-5 (ebook)

PREFACE

There is an old saying, "Wherever you go, there you are." I've been lucky enough to enjoy the thrill and excitement of running rapids on some of America's greatest rivers. And on every rafting trip I've run, people have brought their lives, thoughts, and biases with them. As those who have taken these trips know, the physical and psychological thrills and dangers of a white-water adventure swiftly replace the cares of everyday life.

My purpose is to put you, the reader, on the river with spray in your face, apprehension in your resolve, and a thrill in your heart. If you have never floated down a swollen river, this story will transport you to a new world of exhilaration and adventure. If you're an old salt on the river, hang on tight, because you'll need to look into your tool box of tricks to make it to the end.

As the pace of life shifts on the river, the conversations also change, often to issues that are of great importance to those on the trip. I have experienced, firsthand, many of the conversations that happen in *The Purple River*, and I am struck by the passion and intensity we as individuals hold about the future of our country and our world. There is nothing like taking a brief postponement from your hot debate on climate issues, so you can run Gunslinger Rapid.

ACKNOWLEDGMENTS

The first thanks go to the great team at ScreenShot Publishers for sharing my vision for this book. Special thanks to the river runners who ran the rapids with me all these years. Thanks to Orange Torpedo River Adventures for welcoming us every year and to Arizona Raft Adventures for two great runs down the Grand Canyon. Thanks to Amanda Glaze for taking a chance on kayaking and joining me for the Salmon River trip and for never taking anything I say at face value, but requiring proof for everything. Thanks to Georgia Glaze for making each trip a delight.

1

I waited with Jordan in the flat water above while the first group cleared the rapid. Devin, our guide, paddled vigorously as he hit and pierced the first small wave. With a slight back paddle, he jerked the front of his boat so he would hit the next wave at a right angle. The bow of the air-filled craft punched through the short standing wave, and with a swift stroke on each side, he accelerated through into the quiet water.

Simon spun out just above the rapid, and while he was recovering, the fast current carried Pat past him into the first wave. The curl hit his bow, peppering his face with spray, while starting to roll the boat back to the right. Pat leaned into the wave, thrust his paddle forward and jerked it toward him, leveling his boat as he burst through to the flat water. With a hard stroke on his right side, he accelerated toward the next target. Like Devin, he back paddled on the left, hitting the next wave at a perpendicular angle. Ripping through it, Pat raised his paddle, opened his mouth, and gave a "rebel yell" that echoed through the river canyon.

Meanwhile, regaining control above the rapid, Simon turned his boat downstream to hit the first swell, dead-on. The puny wave was no match for his 240 pounds, and it flattened like an insignificant ripple under his weight. Looking pleased and confident, he steered his boat into the second wave. His broad shoulders and torso, which carried most of his weight, unsettled the boat's balance, and the top-heavy craft lurched to the right. Simon's gut reactions was to lean away from the wave, but that helped tip the boat into the current. The boat rolled and gently laid him into its soft, wet trough.

The current swept Kyle's boat into the rapids behind Simon. As he punched through the first wave, the current thrust the soft rubber bow of his boat into Simon's boat, lodging snuggly into the center of the capsizing craft. The calm water of the trough kept Kyle above water for a second or two as both boats moved into the pounding curl of the small wave. Like Simon, Kyle was laid into the water as if a mother were placing her baby in a warm bath. But even the small wave had enough momentum under the surface to shove both men to the frigid river bottom. They cleared the swirling undertow and popped up like corks, clad in crimson life jackets, about six feet downstream.

Devin grabbed the shoulder panels of Simon's jacket as he surfaced amid the swirling currents and tugged the deadweight of Simon's drenched body over the front of his own boat with ease. Another river guide floated alongside with Simon's boat and helped him settle into the small seat.

"What the hell were you doing up there?" Kyle shouted. "You almost killed me!" He was back in his boat, the current propelling him toward Simon and Devin. He turned his head as he passed to maintain eye contact with Simon. "This is supposed to be a vacation, not a funeral. Look, if you can't cut it, stay out of my way."

Simon was still gasping for air, savoring each precious breath. "Should I give him the finger or just paddle over and bash the little twerp's head in? It might put him out of his misery and do the world a big favor."

Tumbling into the cold, choppy water had utterly disoriented him. He was unnerved, but Simon, who usually paused before he spoke, was not the kind of man to be browbeaten. He was mostly bald, with a well-oiled combover. The bones of his cranium formed small canyons and plateaus, and the back part of his head flattened in a diagonal plain to the ground. His coloring was dark, and his face was clean shaven.

"Let it go," called a voice from just upriver. Pat floated into view from behind Simon. "He wears his emotions on his sleeve. He's just a little jumpy, that's all. Kyle is a client of mine. He's okay," Pat said with cordial resolve.

"I can let it go, Pat, but that guy needs to mellow out or it will be a long week."

"He will," Pat replied. "Everybody mellows out on the river after a few days."

"I hope you're right." Simon paused and began to paddle slowly. "But anyway, these dinky little blowup kayaks aren't exactly my ticket. I mean, they feel top heavy and unstable."

"Well, they're not the best for pros, but they're probably the best for our level."

"Best for what? They're flimsy and cheap."

"But you don't have to know how to roll in the rapids," I said, "because you can't get stuck in the boat, just thrown out."

"Yeah, I noticed," Simon said. "You know, when Pat

said river trip, I thought he meant this would be like my trip down the Grand Canyon. I mean, seven paddlers in a raft digging into those massive curls. I've seen the front guys take the brunt of two giant waves in close succession and get leveled onto the floor of the raft and lucky not to be thrown out and swimming. But everyone else is there to keep digging, so you take whatever the river can throw at you and learn to beat the old matron at her own game." I looked over to the side and saw a quiet river streaming past a steep muddy bank. Mostly young saplings gazed out on the river's constant rush to the sea. The roots of one ancient oak punched through the dirty bank, penetrating the humid air and curving like a giant elbow back down into the current. It looked like a wise old gentleman among a free-for-all of youth. But of course, it wasn't. It was just an old tree surviving in a rugged wilderness.

Why Simon was calling the river a "her" was beyond me. Was it for the same reason hurricanes were named after females? Maybe it was once thought of as a compliment? Or maybe it was a character trait reflected in the big storm, as in "there is no wrath like a woman's scorn." But I remembered that old song about the Mississippi River, *Old Man River*. I guess the Mississippi is a big slow river that "just keeps rollin' along," but the

Grand Canyon has the wrath of a woman, and likewise there would be some trouble on this stretch of the smaller Salmon River. Wrath we could take, I mused; mayhem is harder.

I paddled downriver and caught up with Jordan. As my boat pulled up from behind, I saw her poised demeanor, and the even, steady stroke of her paddling. She was the kind of woman I wish I had met in my youth.

But then I stopped; I knew better than to fool myself. Back then, I was looking for meaning, depth, and sensitivity. I dated girls who were artists and poets and, as it turns out, were mostly tortured by their emotions and the suffering of various populations around the world, just like a poet is supposed to be. Karen, the girl I married, was an artist, completely the opposite of Jordan. She was a good companion and did well with the kids, but her idea of recreation was having tea and chatting. She had a close circle of friends and was reluctant to expand her group. I liked a little broader reach and had friends and also a lot of acquaintances, people I would hang out with but didn't really know. All the same, I was happy with the few friends Karen had and the "good" friendships she kept up. But I was a different person back then, before Karen's passing.

"Hi there," I said, trying to be low-key and easygoing.

"Well, we're off. It should be exciting." "You're Jackson, right?"

I nodded.

"Yeah, it'll be fun if the boys don't kill each other," Jordan replied.

"So you heard the little altercation?"

"Not the whole thing, but I got the general picture. What is the old saying, 'wherever you go, there you are'?" "Yeah, give it a little time," I said. "They'll start playing nice. They've all been out on rivers before."

Jordan looked ahead and quietly paddled her kayak, floating down with the slow-moving current. Her eyes stayed downriver until she turned her head and, in a gentle, quiet voice, like the rhythm of the river, answered, "I have never been on a river trip where I thought everybody on it should be there, or that everybody understood the level of extreme sport this is. It's like a hurricane—the river can be unforgiving and indiscriminate, and good times can go bad quick."

And like a woman, I thought, you want to enjoy its beauty but give it constant respect. I had heard of catastrophes and helicopter evacuations on these trips but had never seen one. We all expected some big waves creating "holes" that could suck you down before spitting you back out to the surface. Some people expected it more than others. But everybody would be fine, I thought.

2

A hundred miles east in the Bitterroot Mountain Range separating Idaho from Montana, a thundercloud blocked out the sun and turned a cool summer morning into nearly night. Summer storms are common in the mountains, where the rainfall can reach sixty inches a year, but this weather front covered one hundred fifty miles north to south and promised a real soaking. The mountain range between the little towns of Salmon, Idaho, and Butte, Montana, are rugged, desolate, and claim only two or three people per square mile. The weather in this remote area is of little interest around the state, and the news reports barely mentioned the storm.

The runoff started in the high mountain canyons as flows so small you could hardly call them streams, but each trickle of water joined a nearby colleague to form narrow torrents that cut through the hilly crevices, giving in to gravity's pull to lower ground. Allan Mountain and Pyramid Peak are both more than nine thousand feet high, and the rain slipped off the mountain surfaces like butter off a hot knife. To the east on the Montana side, the South Fork of the Bitterroot River flowed north, meeting up with the Flathead River, all dumping into Flathead Lake. The flow to the west found the Salmon River, which drains fourteen thousand square miles of wilderness. The Middle Fork joins the Main after a hundred and six miles through one of the deepest gorges in North America. One inch of rain in the mountains can cause these rivers to rise two feet downstream. The rain started about eight thirty in the morning and pelted the mountains with two inches of liquid sunshine in the first hour.

3

The sandy knoll stretched up from the water's edge at a lazy bend in the river. Thirty feet inland, there was a stand of scruffy trees that shaded the fine, cream-colored sand from the burning July sun. I alternated paddle strokes on the right and then left, pausing after each pull of the blade, mostly letting the current take me down the wide, calm stretch.

For our first day, I counted five class two and one class three rapids. The class threes have the big holes, which are two- or three-foot crevices that form directly in front of a standing wave. The waves curl back into the river in an upstream direction, forming a wall of water. The lightweight kayaks we rode sunk into the hole and, if navigated correctly and with enough force, punched through the curl to the water beyond.

On this first day, Kyle made it through the top of the first Class 3, but was off-balance and tippy. Turning sideways, he fell out and rode the rest of it in a cold shiver next to his boat. Simon ran two of the Class 2s well but swam the rest involuntarily, and when his boat beached on the sandbar, he looked spent and exhausted. The cold water and fear of another swim down the rapids was evident in his almost lifeless frame sprawled on the beach. The guides, led by Devin, explained the general strategy before each run but clearly thought it was easier to dredge the fallen boaters out of the rapids and put them back into their boats than to make everybody a sudden expert river rat. I had followed Pat down most of the big ones and copied him as much as I could, so I made it through the afternoon dry and in pretty good shape.

As my boat approached the shore, I saw Pat standing on the sandy beach, winding up for an underhand pitch. "Take a load off with this, big guy." From Pat's hand a sparkling projectile accelerated toward me with precision aim befitting a great athlete. My hands let the paddle drop to the gunnels of my boat, and I instinctively reached over my head with my right hand and plucked the silver bullet from its parabolic flight path. As I brought it down, my left hand found the pull top and I yanked open the first beer of the day, a much-deserved reward. Pat gave a mild yell. Kyle shrugged. Jordan ignored it, and Simon, after briefly standing, again collapsed on the sand.

4

Pat was my roommate in college and one of the most outgoing guys in the fraternity. While he was not the face man in the house, he could charm the chrome off a trailer hitch. He was an economics major but filled his electives with philosophy courses that he rarely talked about except after a lot of beer, and even then, he couldn't get much conversation going because nobody else in the fraternity ever went near a philosophy course. Over the last twenty years, he built a huge business as a stockbroker in Hollywood, but he liked to stay light about life. Every few months I'd get a call from him.

"Hey, big guy, how is the young, nubile talent count around town these days?" he would ask.

We hung on to the lingo of our fraternity days, not

because we lived it anymore or because Pat or I took any interest in the "eye candy," but because we got to escape for a few seconds to a time we could never replace and weren't all that happy to let go.

"Have you been river rafting since your Grand Canyon trip a few years ago?" he asked.

"Been thinking about it, but I never have carved out the time," I replied. "Do I sense a proposition coming on?"

"I've got a client who is a nut for river trips. Anyway, he went down the middle fork of the Salmon River last summer and is completely worked up about going down the main fork this year. He's putting together a small private trip with a guide service from the local area, but this time it's in one-man kayaks. Interested?"

"Is that in Montana?" I asked. "Close, buddy-boy. It's in Idaho." "Where's Idaho, anyway?" I quipped.

"It's about four hours by plane and about two weeks by mule train, smartass."

I loved it when Pat called. We had a storehouse of inside jokes that never got old.

"Seen Muffin lately?" he would ask.

"No, but I can smell the aroma of that lovely flower around every corner."

And we would both break out in garish hilarity—

over what? Over nothing, just the thought of Muffin, a party queen who hung around the frat house for our last two years. She was just a girl back then, but now she was a symbol of the way we were, and would never be again. It would be just a phone call, and it was always over too soon.

Pat's friend, Kyle, took care of all the logistics and organized the trip. He was a biology professor at the University of California in Riverside. Pat's clients all have small fortunes, and with his professor's salary, Kyle would hardly be in that category. But around ten years ago, he wrote a book about global warming that took off like a shot. It was perfect timing, because the issue started getting front-page coverage in major media just about that time. He made millions and became a poster-boy for the cause. The guy was on TV for a year, it seemed, and on the lecture circuit—he was the star du jour.

That book was considered pivotal because it outlined the primary concepts of the movement of global warming. Back then it was a worst-case scenario of a group of computer models generated in "what if" situations, but Kyle's book took the worst case and turned it into the "only case," and slowly the theory became a fact. The whole idea of sunlight trapped by a layer of pollution seemed reasonable to me. Global temperature variations on the planet, and the history of these cycles, is a field I know nothing about, but the global warming thing just might have substance.

Kyle was low-key about his success, but his general nature was high-strung and argumentative. Pat made sure everybody knew how to get along with him. All the guys had been briefed, and everybody seemed cool about it.

Simon had some history with Pat running rivers, and he was an affable guy with a big heart. Born in Iran, he moved to Seattle at the age of ten when his father landed a job in the aerospace industry at Boeing. Right after, the U.S.-friendly Shah of Iran was overthrown, and the radical religious sects took control of the country. According to Pat, Simon went back to Iran a few times as an adult, but they must have been secret trips because he never talked about the details.

An oncologist specializing in ovarian cancer in Los Angeles, Simon was in a private practice with five doctors. His affiliation with the UCLA Medical Center brought him into contact with Pat as a financial advisor. Simon was jovial and easygoing with a hyena cackle of a laugh that some people thought was infectious, but I always thought sounded a little forced or fabricated. He was a good guy, don't get me wrong, but like everybody, I figured Simon had some onion-skin layers concealing deep secrets.

The big wildcard for the trip was Jordan. She was a friend of Simon's daughter, Alicia, and the two of them were signed on for the trip. Alicia, however, had to cancel because of a bad tennis accident two days before the trip. The assumption was that Jordan wouldn't want to spend a week floating down the river with a bunch of middle-aged guys who were old enough to be her father, but when the group arrived at the airport in Los Angeles, there she was, quietly waiting and ready to go.

Simon knew her because she had hung out with Alicia a few times at his backyard swimming pool. He had been extremely reluctant to go himself, because Alicia's injuries were severe. She was a tennis pro at the Bel-Air Country Club. During a warm-up game, she charged the net to return a volley. Her feet tangled and she crashed onto the court, shattering her elbow and fracturing her knee. Simon's wife, who never went on outdoor adventures with him, convinced everybody she had everything under control, and even Alicia insisted that Simon and Jordan both go.

Jordan was thirty-four, with an MBA from the

Anderson School of Business at UCLA, and a political journalist for the *American Patriot*, a conservative weekly periodical. She was single and appeared to be very happy with that—comfortable in her own skin, so to speak. Standing five-feet, four-inches, she had an attractive, outdoorsy haircut, a thin straight nose that looked a little Scandinavian, and fair skin dotted with a few small freckles on the edge of her high cheeks.

The first time I saw her, she was standing in the back of a crowded bar in Salmon, Idaho. I flew in from San Francisco and had just arrived by cab from the small airport, fresh in on a puddle jumper from Boise, and I had no idea she was going down the river with us.

The L.A. group had been there a couple of hours when I strolled into the watering hole. A light mounted on the wall illuminated the right side of her face, and her profile was striking, almost taking my breath away. After greeting Pat and the others, I tried to work my way over to her, figuring I'd never see her again, but Kyle buttonholed me to talk about real estate investing as she slipped out the front door and disappeared.

5

Devin meandered into the light of the campfire. He was looking around, probably for Jordan, I thought. There was no doubt he had noticed her. They were about the same age, and let's face it, that's where the chemistry is. I glanced up from my hamburger and baked beans to see him tucking a small guitar under his right arm. He strummed a chord.

"'Kumbaya,' anyone?" he said with a sheepish grin. At five feet, five inches, he was svelte and muscular.

His short, brown hair had an unkempt wilderness look, with fashionable sideburns extending below his ears. Nine summers guiding river trips had turned his skin a dark bronze tone, which glowed in the light of the dancing flames. Devin entertained for half an hour with campfire songs. When he strummed "I'm An Old Cow Hand from the Rio Grande," one of the guides pulled a box of strike- matches out of his pocket and began shaking them to the song's beat. My foot patted out the rhythm as I settled into a welcomed slow groove.

The large birch log I sat on must have washed up during some high-water rainy season in the last decade or so. Smooth knobs were all that remained of once-majestic branches long ago broken off and honed by a relentless river flow. The furrowed exterior was split by long cracks running its length and traversing the white, sun-bleached surface. Dead lichen clung to the shat-tered ends like old glue. Mine was not the only polished log anchored to the shore. The small ones got thrown on the fire, but the big ones rooted out a lifeless founda-tion in the sand where they could rest and watch the world unfold.

When the song ended, Kyle said in a low voice, "It's good to be in the wilderness and out of California."

"Yeah, the quiet out here is deafening," I said, more to the red-glowing fire than to Kyle. Tomorrow is the third day out of the city, I thought, and the three-day rule always works. Three days to unwind. I could feel the dull buzz of civilization fading away. The subtle sounds of the river at night were becoming more vivid. Wilderness was the right place to be. I was almost me again. Nobody's calling me "sir," no meetings to run or bankers to cajole. Just paddle myself down the river on my own and everybody else would take care of themselves.

I was so overwhelmed with delight that I leaned over as far as I could, reached into the ice chest and pulled out another beer. Here's to day three, I thought.

Kyle pierced my tranquility. "It's really good to get away from all the mess that's happening everywhere." He paused. "Sorry for being a downer, but...well you know. You guys keep up with the nonstop terrible news everywhere. I guess everybody needs a break, right?"

I could tell the buzz in Kyle's ears was more like a vise around his head. He might need three weeks to unwind.

"What did you think of our first day on the river, Kyle?" I said, trying to change the subject back to a more pleasant topic. The water was gently slapping the sandbar,

and the night air was cooling rapidly.

Ignoring my question, he said, "I mean, there are fanatics everywhere."

I wondered if I should make one more attempt to

change the subject, or just find my tent and crash. Kyle was an okay guy, but I didn't escape civilization to wallow in world problems.

A voice from behind me pierced the brief silence: "Well, the problems are manmade and they've got to be solved by people."

Kyle looked over his left shoulder and saw Jordan standing in the faint light of the low smoldering fire.

"Where did you come from?" he said slightly under his breath, an irritated grimace on his face. His chin dropped as his head turned toward the fire.

I looked up away from the fire and could see the dense cloud cover blanketing most of the night sky. Low in the west, the clouds broke slightly, and the three stars that formed the top of Orion's belt peeked through. My mind fixed for half a second on a sense of the big picture, the beginning and the end, not just the details in the middle, ideas that a determined businessman running his own company has little time for back home.

Devin jumped in front of the fire, pulled his guitar up under his arm and strummed a few chords. Faint lightning flashes illuminated the cloud cover in the eastern sky. It looked like a storm was going to unleash itself on the eastern mountain range. Maybe it wouldn't come over this far, but we could handle some rain on the river if it did. It just meant the sun wouldn't be drying us off and warming us up.

Everybody was silent for a brief moment, and I could hear the river flowing. The steady sound of the water settled my mind. During the winter when it rained more often, I guessed that the sound was different, maybe a higher-pitched roar. The steady droning sound of the water bouncing off the rocks and the riverbanks probably sounded the same when Caesar crossed the Rubicon in 6 BC, and when Washington crossed the Delaware in 1776. Kyle broke the calm. "Look guys, I've spent a career working on the most crucial problem facing our planet, global warming brought on by pollution. Corporations were polluting the drinking water, the air, and the ocean at a devastating pace before the environmental movement started. And we need this movement. If fossil fuel emission continues at this rate, the planet will heat the ice caps and flood the major continents in ten years. Kiss civilization good-bye."

Devin interjected, "I've read some scary stuff about the polar ice caps, affected by pollution from smoke-stacks and cars."

"Carbon emissions are increasing as more countries industrialize," Kyle added.

"Mostly from cars, right? Electricity is clean?" Devin asked.

"Cars are a big part of it, but power plants producing electricity put a lot of carbon in the atmosphere," Kyle responded.

"But most new electric plants in the U.S. these days are natural-gas fired," Jordan chimed in, "so they burn cleaner."

"Okay, Jordan, listen carefully. I'm going to give you a little lesson in economics straight from the world of hard knocks," Kyle said slowly with a hint of sarcasm. "Power plants are mostly built to use the fuel source that is most available and most economical in that particular region. Transportation is very advanced in the developed countries, so pipelines carry oil and gas around the U.S. and Canada. But in China, for example, where the economic growth is so rapid and transportation is less developed, plants are being rushed into service in areas where coal is the only plentiful energy source. Factories are producing everything from can openers to iPods, and the population is demanding a higher lifestyle. This translates into more gadgets that run on electricity. Smokestacks are billowing carbon into the atmosphere in order to keep up with electricity demand."

"But the scientific reality is, it may be air pollution, but it's hard to relate that directly to climate change," Jordan said.

Simon jumped into the conversation. "The climate has been changing for centuries, long before smokestacks."

"So what!" Pat said. "I can't see why filling the atmosphere with this much pollution is an acceptable thing anyway."

"The coastal cities in the world could be flooded in ten years from polar melting," Kyle said. "Plus, growth in the volume of the oceans just from heat expansion."

"Climate change can't go that quickly," Jordan said. "It's a longer-term cycle."

"This one could," Kyle replied.

The air felt moist as the rain threatened, but Kyle's dire prediction proved the true damp blanket on the conversation. He, by far, was the expert in this field, and there wasn't much effort to take it any further. It was quiet for a while, and I could feel Kyle basking in the glory of his triumph. *El professor* had spoken. I thought the heavy topics were over for the night, and hopefully for the rest of the trip, but Kyle was on a roll and wanted to take advantage of his position to make a few essential points for our nightcap.

I sat there like a statue transfixed by the conversation, but even in the low firelight, I could see Kyle's face turning red. Kyle and Jordon were gearing up for some fireworks, and Kyle was going to be the first one to blow, I thought.

"If you take a ninety-minute movie and show thirty seconds of it, you can't really know what the movie is about," Jordan said. "If you take twenty years out of a 250,000-year climate cycle, you can't really make a meaningful analysis."

"To Kyle's point, when we were growing up, big companies didn't take any responsibility for their waste or pollution," I said. "I, for one, am glad we have a new group running these companies and we have cleaner air and water."

"Well, they didn't do it on their own. I can promise you that," Kyle said. "Hard-won battles by a dedicated group both in and out of the government brought about laws that protect everybody. Hell, the government was dumping nuclear waste in the Pacific Ocean. What were they thinking?"

"It takes a different mindset to do manufacturing, and all business for that matter, in a clean, responsible way. But once that mindset is established, it becomes more a question of how to do business cleanly, not whether you do it cleanly," I said.

"It's naïve to think that big business will follow through on its own," Kyle said. "They have to be made to conform. Corporate titans have one thing on their minds: profit, and that always comes at the expense of the average citizen. Everybody knows that."

He stood up when he said "corporate titan" and slowly paced in front of the fire. Having regained his ground, his delivery was professorial and confident, and his voice notched down to a lower register as he bent down and picked up a small log. He held it in front of him just below his line of vision. As he finished talking, his eyes dropped slightly, and he studied the log's craggy surface before tossing it into the center of the fire pit. The sun-dried log nuzzled a berth for itself in the red-hot bed of burning coals but did not immediately start to blaze, while meandering funnels of gray smoke cut a channel around it and up through the dancing flames and escaped to the night sky.

Jordan rose from her perch on a large, rounded bolder but changed her mind and sat back down. She shifted her right hip forward on the rock and seemed to find a more comfortable position. But I sensed she was not going to find any comfort in this conversation with Kyle. Devin jumped up, gave a cordial but understated nod to the group, and disappeared into the darkness. For an instant, I thought there would be a rebuttal from Jordan, but she sat back and let the peace and tranquility of our rustic environs prevail.

Then the low clouds lit up as a sharp thunderclap stopped Kyle in mid-sentence. The cracking blast shook the ground and a downpour of cold, driving rain began. Jordan pulled her collar around her neck and flipped the hood over her head. She leaped off the rock with both feet landing on the ground at the same time. Her right foot took a step around the rock, and by the time her left foot and the rest of her body caught up, she had vanished into the black night.

Kyle and I moved quickly toward the tents, but at the pace of middle-aged men with more to move and less agility to propel us. There was no camaraderie or acknowledgement between us about our declining mobility. No nodding. No winks. It was raining too hard. We just ran.

6

The rain pounded on the tent walls and seemed to wash away the contentious campfire debate from my mind. I crawled into the sleeping bag fully clothed, shifted down until it covered my cold, shivering shoulders. Slowly, thoughts of last summer jumped into my head. I'd been in Jamaica, a last-minute trip by myself just to get away from the city. What a different place than this riverbank, hot and lush from twelve months of rain, but the most striking difference was the poverty in Jamaica.

Outside the rain fell harder. I looked up into the pitch- black tent, which gave no suggestion of my whereabouts as I felt my body gradually relax, my eyes close. I fell into a deep sleep and dreamed.

"*Pick a spot on that rock and stare at it. You might stay balanced if you keep your eyes focused,*" I said to myself, leaning and shaky. "*Try lifting the right foot; dip it in the mini-pool of rushing water. Fast. Dry your bare foot with the towel, stick it in the sandal quickly before you fall over. Keep your eye on that spot, on the rock, on one foot, in the water.*"

Both sandals on my feet, dry, no sand, pretty good. The water was refreshing but not too cool, about eighty degrees. The pool caught and accumulated the water from the falls. Handmade, head-sized rocks stacked and capped off with bags of small stones formed a dam to hold the water.

Through a thumb-size hole in the top of one of the bags of rocks, I could see the stones were a variety of colors with edges rounded by thousands of years of work from the hand of God. The bathers crawled over the top of the bags into the waist- high pool. They were flailing, frolicking, and splashing. About three at a time fit under the falls as it plunged a modest thirty feet onto the heads and shoulders of the swimmers, pounding their heads as the price for the cool massage down their shoulders. The winding riverbed below the pool drained out and through the last several miles of the Blue Mountains into the warm Caribbean Sea.

I lifted my head, opened one eye, and pulled myself up onto my right elbow. Reaching with my left hand, I found the tent wall. "I'm on the river, dreaming about Jamaica," I said to myself as my heavy eyelids fell once more and my head again found the makeshift pillow.

"Hey, mon, you buy some mangos, two hundred J," he shouted as he strolled in my direction. Next to the fruit stand there was a shack made of corrugated tin, indistinguishable from the hundreds of others all over Jamaica.

A contraption that looked like a combination of a chicken cage, a vegetable strainer, a violin bow, and an ice cream maker with a crank handle sat in a little Flexible Flyer wagon on the weather-beaten wood.

"No mangos for me today. How did you make this?" I asked as I pointed to the fantastic machine. I thought to ask what it did or who it did it to, but stopped short.

A quiet, bored, and slightly unsettled look came over his face as he quietly uttered, "Turn-hand-make-fashion."

My blank stare did not catch him by surprise. Even though a simple roadside warrior, he seemed accustomed to talking to "whites." My eye wandered to the dry riverbed behind the tin shack, where the scorched sand and rocks shrugged off the broken-bottle-tin-can population covering it, and it looked fresh and vibrant and decades old at the same time. The array of debris, old and new, was not litter or trash. It lay there as a necessary part of the environment, part of now, part of my mango seller's life. Even if somebody tried to clean it up, the cluttered riverbed wouldn't go away. The litter would reappear. It belonged there.

"You take what you got and make what you want," he said, explaining himself.

The late-night TV blared the news. From slits in my eyelids, I could see her behind the news desk, the nice-looking bouncy blonde, like all the other blondes.

"Half the marriages in the U.S. end in divorce. It's because the river is too deep, it's too wide, it's too cold, it's too hot, it's too clean, it's too dirty. The river is too vast. There is too much potential, and the handbook is out of print. When the music stops, do you have a chair? Get your chair early and marry your high school sweetheart. Get her quick before she disappears. There is a two-for-one sale at Walmart on the fourth of July, no handbook required."

I rolled over in my sleeping bag, opening one eye at a time, and looked at the top of the tent just three feet above my head. The faint light of the morning sun shone through the waterproof fabric that looked almost dry from the inside. The rain had stopped for now. The only sound was the steady drone of the river. Then the whole tent started shaking.

"Get that fishing pole, buddy. Let's catch some breakfast." I crawled out with my fishing rod and the small box of flies I bought from the hole-in-the-wall fly shop on Union Street in San Francisco.

"Where's the coffee, Davy?" I tossed out. "Davy?" Pat said.

"Davy Crockett. Get with the program," I said while straightening my rain parka.

"Oh yeah, Davy Crockett," he replied. "Anyway, coffee is for wimps, and you won't need those flies."

"Okay, we're going to catch them with our hands, right?" I said.

"That's how I usually do it, but in case that doesn't work, I bought these local flies in the sports shop in Salmon next to the motel. Local caddis and even fat nymphs if we can't talk them into rising."

"I was counting on that," I replied. "Did you bring the tartar sauce?"

"Tartar sauce is for wi—"

"I know, is for wimps," I said.

We walked downstream along the riverbank for a few hundred yards until Pat found an eddy in the river and positioned himself near a steep overhang on the bank that looked like a hiding place for wild trout. I watched the fast-moving water in the middle of the river. It curled back to the right and flowed upstream in a circular movement to form the eddy, before settling on a spot where the riverbank jutted five feet out at the lower end. Indeed, a little cover under the overhang, deep enough to keep it cold, close to the fast water for food supply and relief from the current. A few small ripples formed on the side of the eddy where caddis, nymphs, and other food fell out of the river flow. Big trout can rest there from the current and feed easily. Good fishing here.

I pulled my rod out of the hard-shell case and slid the reel onto it just above the cork handle. Tying a caddis fly on the end of the leader line, I squeezed out a drop of floatation liquid onto my forefinger and thumb and stroked the artificial bait, careful not to spear my skin with the razor-sharp barb. I whipped the rod a few times in the air to draw out the line and let it fall into the water upstream from the targeted overhang.

Whipping the rod tip again I mended the feeder line upstream, assuring the fly would float down at the natural speed of the current and waited as the slow current of the eddy moved the fly into range of the rising fish. Looking across the river, I saw the early-morning light cut through the narrow canyon and gently layer itself on the crystal water. The reflection of the red sun and the cotton sky painted a color pallet on the canvas of yellow, orange, and purple. This was the third day, the buzz had vacated my ears, and my liberation from civilization was all but assured. Suddenly muffled voices broke my quiet communion with the river.

"...they're not easy to catch," Pat explained. "It looks like it's about the rod and the reel and the flies, but it's not. It's more about a quiet mind. A quiet mind allows you to be part of nature. You have to be still to understand how to be part of nature."

Jordan said in a respectfully low voice, "Nature isn't all that benign, Pat. Survival is a struggle for all species."

It looked like Jordan had run into Pat while taking an early-morning stroll.

"What I mean," Pat continued, "is that you can't skate off the information super highway onto the back roads of the wilderness and catch a fish with a fly rod. You have to take the time to relearn things. There has to be a rebirthing in your mind to get in sync with nature."

"Well, I appreciate the Zen of it all," Jordan said, "but we are here and we are eating food from the supermarket and drinking the beer you guys brought and sleeping in tents that came from Sports Authority. None of this is exactly spun from nature. I guess cell phones don't work out here, but the information highway is right around the next bend."

"Yeah, but I'm talking about catching a fish with a fly rod. This part of nature has its own scale, its own rhythm. You can't be part of the workaday world and expect to be one with an ecosystem as intimate as this one. There is a group of organisms that live to reproduce once and die. The mayfly is one of these animals. Its larvae are deposited on the bottom of a river. The nymph forms and moves to the mid-depths. At this stage it is known as a midge. As it reaches the surface, it's called a cadis or mayfly. It looks like the mayfly lands on the water, but it actually just floats to the top. Then to dry its wings, it flaps them frantically in the air. This movement drives the trout crazy, and it can lead to a feeding frenzy. After it leaves the water's surface, the fly will mate in midair and drop back to the water, again attracting the trout. It all happens in a short period of time, and the fish feed on them during every stage."

Jordan was sitting on a stump about five feet from Pat. Her eyes followed the movement of his fly rod as his right arm heaved the pole over his shoulder. The fly whipped back at the end of the leader line once, twice, three times and onto the river. Each time more line pulled out of the reel, his casting motion slowed, but each time the exaggerated movement threw more line out from the rod, extending the reach of the bait. The brown fuzzy food floated with the slow current into the feeding area.

Finally Jordan asked, "Are you at one with the fish or the fly?"

"There is always a point in nature when you don't hear a sound, a short time when you are sitting and the birds don't chirp and the wind doesn't rustle the trees. That's a window into nature. The silences in nature are the doorways into a secret world." After a moment, he finally answered, "Both."

Pat always seemed so happy-go-lucky, but there was a quiet depth to him that he rarely revealed. He caught three sizable fish and carefully put each one back in the river. I had one strike from a monster rainbow, but he stripped the barb-less hook and got away. Jordan resumed her hike, and Pat and I meandered back to camp.

"What's the deal on Jordan?" I asked. "She was going head-to-toe with Kyle last night around the campfire."

"She's a cute package. Knows her mind," Pat replied.

"She could be a hard one to handle, especially if your politics are wrong."

The conversation dropped off as we walked toward the camp. The morning sun peaked through a broken cloud cover, taking the edge off the crisp morning air. The soggy, rain-drenched grass just off the path rustled from the movement of some brand of crawling resident, but neither Pat nor I reacted. We just walked quietly.

Finally, Pat broke the silence.

"You ought to try to get to know her. It's time you hooked up with somebody to take your mind off that lousy golf game of yours."

"Yeah, well, I banked the six bucks last time we played, Mr. Cool," I answered. "I could get a crush on her if I tried. What do you think? Think it'd be child molesting?" I queried with a joke, but hoping he would take the inference seriously and give me some advice.

"She's younger, but there's no child inside that skin. I think you should go slow and see if there's any meeting of the minds. That's 'minds,' buddy-boy. Keep the other parts out of it for now."

"So you don't think the Conan the Barbarian technique will work with her?"

"You're lame with women, as usual, Conan."

7

The rain started a slow, steady drizzle as we tried to finish breakfast. I quickly abandoned the open-air dining hall and crawled in my tent, laid on my stomach, and planted my elbows symmetrically in front of me, giving my hands and forearms free movement. I then ungracefully cleaned my plate. Just then came a booming voice.

"Listen up, everybody! It's a wet one, so roll those sleeping bags up, stuff 'em in your dry-bag inside your tent. Try to keep it all dry. Today is a good day for the paddle jackets, and wet suits can be picked up at the supply boat if you want one. This is a day that will put hair on your chests, boys. And yes, women, it will put hair on your chests too. His voice held the authority of a seasoned leader. "Remember, it doesn't do any good to fall in. You get just as wet on top of the river today."

I finished my packing and slipped through the narrow tent opening. The rain was falling lightly, and the low cloud cover was blocking any direct view of the sun. I looked toward Jordan's tent to see how she was managing her gear in the rain.

I walked around to the back of my tent and loosened the two metal stakes I had driven into the sand. They held well last night, even in the face of some strong gusts. I looked up to see Jordan's dry-bag fly out of her tent. It hit the soggy sand and rolled over once before settling in a small puddle.

She stepped out, looked over her shoulder at me, and said, "Let's get these tents down to the boats. Come on, let's do yours first."

I threw the stakes on the sand beside my tent and folded the top onto the side as evenly as I could. Jordan took the front of the tent and lifted it up while I lifted the back. We folded the right side and then the left into the center. She bent the front into two-foot lengths toward the back, careful to brush the sand off as she went.

After taking her tent down, she grabbed both and took off to the supply boat before I could offer to help.

The rain slacked off as I picked up our dry-bags and looked at the kayaks lined up neatly on the beach. Jordan trotted back up the hill, and I held out her bag for her to take as we walked down to the water.

"Were you okay with Devin's comment this morning?" I asked.

"About the rain?" she asked with a questioning look. "About the hair on the chest," I clarified.

Jordan took a deep breath as a gentle wind blew up the river canyon, cooling the beads of rain on my face. I shifted the strap of my dry-bag up higher on my shoulder and straightened my back to accommodate the added weight. Jordan moved her left arm across her body and took the handle of her bag, lifting it from her right shoulder and, in a single motion, letting it drop in front of her.

She stopped and turned to me with the gentlest, almost compassionate look I had seen from her in the three days I had known her. The weight of her body settled back on her heels as she began to explain her message, almost like a teacher showing a young student how to simplify a complex problem.

"People who don't live in the cities sometimes don't know about all this PC stuff," she said. "They live a simpler life where relationships are not as complicated and based more on what they need to do rather than somebody's idea of the way things ought to be. Devin didn't mean anything derogatory; he was just trying to lighten up a tense situation. The dry, river-guide-instruction doesn't always keep people's attention. It's like advertising. If you don't say things in a new, creative way, your message will get lost in the crowd. This is going to be a rough day on the river, and if we see signs of flooding, it could get hairy in these light-weight kayaks. I think a little color in the explanation helps to paint a picture of what we need to be thinking about this morning on this rough river."

"I understand what you mean, and I support the whole women's movement. Women have many more opportunities and are taken more seriously in business and the workplace. Half of my friends played sports on college teams that didn't exist twenty years ago. But that doesn't mean I want to strip the spice out of life. Look, every reference to gender or sex is not an attack. It's fun to spar."

"Yeah, I get that," I said.

"I know women who go around scripting every-body's language," she continued, "and when people don't say things and do things the way they want, they get upset and try to say society is going down the tubes or that the guy is a pig. These women have a flat world, no color and no humor, and I think mostly they're insecure. Devin is not my type, but he's a fun guy, and we may need all the humor we can get today."

The boats were lined up on the beach, and I found one next to Pat. Jordan really made me think about things in a different way. She was far from feminine in the "girly" sense, but her confidence and outdoorsy look made her drop-dead beautiful again this morning. So Devin wasn't her type? Yeah, well, that age was her type. Forget it, I thought. Then I looked up and saw Pat staring at me.

"You bagged out early from the campfire last night," I said nervously. It was the first thing that jumped into my head, and I hoped he hadn't noticed my wistful look.

"Well, I had to get my beauty sleep," he replied while stuffing his gear bag. He knew just what I was thinking, but was letting me off the hook like a good buddy does every now and then.

"Yeah, well, as I said, you didn't miss much, just squabbling about stuff we can't do anything about," I said, trying to keep a little banter going while tying my own gear down.

A gust of wind blew a rolling ripple across the flat

river. I dropped the straps I was holding and pressed down on the bag to hold it onto the boat while I waited for the water to level out.

Maybe she'll forget about your enduring devotion and fall in love with Kyle. That would save us the misery of an ugly debate every night."

I felt my whole body tighten. Conan the Barbarian was not happy with that little quip.

8

Pat shoved off from the shore and fell in behind the group. Walking out until the water lapped just below my knees, I threw myself onto the seat of the boat and, with two firm strokes, pointed the bow upstream into the swift current. The downstream flow caught bow, turned it abruptly to the right, and into the current. One stroke on the left straightened the craft, and I fell in line behind Pat.

The current was faster than yesterday. Small branches and other debris floated aimlessly alongside us. The river bent to the left, and as I cleared the turn, I saw the boats crowding around Devin. Approaching the group, I back paddled on the left and the boat slowed and turned toward the bank and the group. The rain had let up, and the surface of the river was smooth and flat.

Devin started, "Okay, this was a class two yesterday, but it's a class three today. If it keeps raining, it'll be a class five tomorrow, so let's get through this baby now."

Jordan smirked and said in a low voice, "Class five. Come on."

"I thought he was a fun kind of guy," I whispered with a subtle smile.

"Yeah, but class five?" she replied.

"There's a big hole in the middle," he continued, "but you have to hit it from the right side. So, run the rapid down the left bank. Just before that big rock, turn hard right and paddle toward the mouth of the wave. That hard right stroke will turn your boat left, and you'll hit the wave straight on. When—check that—if you fall out, let go of your paddle and float feet-first. The guides will pick you up. Single file and follow me."

Devin turned toward the fast-moving water.

"This is going to be carnage no matter what class this is," Jordan muttered.

Kyle paddled hard to get behind Devin and in front of Simon. I watched as Devin hit the hole, his boat disappearing for an instant as the bow nose-dived into the crevice. Then suddenly, his yellow craft shot up in almost vertical flight. His bow pierced the front of the wave and, reaching forward, he dug his paddle into the face of the curl and pulled back with a fierce motion, causing his boat to blast through to the other side.

He turned hard right and settled his boat in a small, tenuous eddy, waiting to help fish out the would-be swimmers. Kyle followed. As he made it through the wave, he headed straight downstream, taking the current right past Devin. Pat was next while Jordan, Simon, and I waited at the top of the rapid.

Jordan floated up to Simon and said gently, "Stay right behind me and, instead of a hard-right stroke before the hole, give it a nice easy back paddle on the left. That should turn you into the wave just fine. Are you all set?"

Simon gave her a slight nod and said, "Let's go."

He stayed two boat lengths behind her and mirrored her every move. Just before the hole, he dipped his paddle in on the left side and gave the effortless back stroke, as instructed. The boat jutted left into the soft flow of the hole, and as his bow hit the wave, his long arms reached forward to the front of the boat and, with a massive stoke, thrust the craft through the wave.

He accelerated past Devin, raised his paddle above his head with both hands and let out a piercing yell.

Jordan grinned from ear to ear. When Pat and I made it down, Simon raised his paddle again and the whole crew raised their paddles and gave a jubilant cry, knowing they'd beat the river.

We ran a succession of three rapids with no major hurdles, then the water flattened out and we leisurely floated down with the current. The boats spread apart almost in single file. The whole crew seemed to be enjoying the rest and solitude of an easy float down the river. When the sun peeked through the clouds, I could feel the warmth penetrating my paddle jacket.

I heard a *swoosh* of water and then, "You jerk," and something big slapped onto the water's surface.

"You're going to pay, I swear, you *are* going to pay," I heard from behind me.

"Let the games begin," Simon shouted.

I looked back to see Devin sculling his boat in wide circles around a swimming Jordan. She was holding on to the sides of her kayak and her floatation vest kept her shoulders and head above water level. He moved closer and tried to hand her paddle back to her in a tentative gesture. When her fingers touched the paddle, she grabbed the blade and jerked it toward her, trying to snare her opponent.

Devin quickly let go of the blade end and the paddle

dropped to the water as Jordan thrust herself toward his boat. Her hand fell on the right gunnel, trying to get a grip on his craft. Devin's wide grin vanished for a split second as he dipped his paddle into the water, and his easy back paddle pulled the boat away, while Jordan's hand dropped away. Devin's grin reemerged, while Jordan's wide smile betrayed her playful anger. She had been ambushed and thrown into the water, beaten in a playful competition that she didn't know was coming, but she was having a ball. There they go again, I thought. The young crowd.

Devin floated by me, moving to the front of the pack, when Kyle shouted out, "Picking on the girls? Going for the easy targets, I see."

Kyle was trying to be part of the fun, and that friendly gesture would likely get him into the fray. But he had little chance to win a water battle with any of the guides. They spent four months a year on the river paddling these kayaks. The strength in their arms and shoulders allowed them to effortlessly maneuver these boats.

"I can flip that guy like a matchstick," Jordan said as she floated alongside Pat and me. "Girls are easy targets, my ass!"

She looked in good humor but defiant, like a young

horse kicking loose a new saddle, refusing to be broken, determined to keep the rider on his own feet and not on its back. Somehow, she couldn't focus on defeat. Whatever the odds, and they were huge, she only saw herself winning this contest.

River jousting is a huge favorite with kayakers, where competitors stand in their boats and jab at their opponents, trying to knock them off balance. Devin had instigated a surprise attack on Jordan, floating up stealthily behind her, attaining a firm hold on the back of her craft before flipping it and Jordan into the drink. He was a master practitioner of that move, and although she felt the need and the innate ability to dump him in retaliation, she stood little chance of succeeding.

"I see Devin is spreading the humor a little bit, Jordan," I said. "What a guy."

"He'll pay for his indiscretions," said the wild horse. "That grin will fade to blue, just wait."

Kyle spread his feet to the edges of his boat, wedged them in and stood straight up, tenuously preparing to challenge would-be attackers. However, his rudderless kayak quietly entered a small twist in the current and spun end-to-end. With only the river current propelling them, the other boats floated downstream, leaving Kyle and his challenge unanswered. His boat wobbled, and so, close to losing his balance and collapsing into the water, he managed to sit back down without falling in, but remained several hundred yards behind the group.

We continued to float leisurely down the wide slow stretch of river. I caught up with Pat, and he looked over and said, "Maybe she won't be falling in love with either of those guys very soon."

"Give it time," I said. "Good things take time."

I felt my stomach churn a little bit as I spoke those words. A woman like Jordan calls her own shots; she does what she wants and lets the chips fall where they will. So I needed to back off and just watch. Keep my expectations low. Fantasies—those are what get you. You start thinking out ahead of yourself and dreaming of what it might be like, and then the reality never matches the vision.

Slow down, I told myself. After all, this was day three, the office was far away, and all I had to worry about was getting down the next rapid.

Jordan and Simon floated up to me, and the three of us paddled steadily and meticulously down the flat stretch of water not saying a word. A group of four egrets flew lazily overhead, their wings spread wide and fixed in a majestic glide while surveying the river's path from above. I wanted to get some conversation going with Jordan, but nothing seemed right to say. A few quips about how she got dumped in the water by Devin? Wrong. What about Alicia's tennis accident? No good. How about those burgers last night? I couldn't think of a thing. Maybe the women's thing from this morning. She seemed to love arguing political stuff.

I let the lazy current carry us down for a few more minutes. Finally, I looked over at Jordan and said, "Some of these political things can take a life of their own."

"Yeah, a life of its own," she said almost under her breath. "It's like the Vietnam War. Do you know much about that nasty little episode?"

"Well, if being in it counts, I guess I know a little about it. Didn't see combat, though. After it was over, I went to grad school and wanted to get past it as soon as I could." "The dirty truth is that the facts got lost, and the thing took on a life of its own."

"Come on, there were some good reasons to do what we did," I protested.

"Here's the way it went down. An inexperienced President Kennedy faced a hostile Cold War environment, with the Soviet Union literally pounding shoes on the table to proclaim they were going to bury us, while this whole insane nuclear arms race raged on."

"Right. In high school we practiced bombing drills."

"I'll bet you don't forget that."

"No, you don't."

"While the Soviets were trying to convert other countries to communism, we developed the domino theory, which was that if one country fell to the commies, they all would. So, stopping the fall in Vietnam was part of the game. The Kennedy team never planned a war and certainly didn't want to move in U.S. troops because they never, for a second, thought we could win a war in that environment. Then Kennedy was shot, and the new group took over under President Johnson. As the generals and bureaucrats rotated in and out, the institutional memory of the original concept was lost and the mantle of war was taken up by a new, more zealous group each time."

"I don't remember—why didn't Johnson step in to hold these gung-ho guys back?" I asked.

"That was the sad part. Johnson did a political trade with the war hawks in Congress. If they voted for his

War on Poverty programs, he would push the Vietnam War forward. It worked great for those guys, but it was a bad deal for everyone else."

"Then President Nixon came along."

"Nixon entered office with a war-torn electorate and a failing conflict in Southeast Asia. He found a way to end the whole thing within a couple of years, thank God."

"I guess that really did take on its own life," I said. "Yup, it did, but that's what happens all over. I see it in businesses I cover for my magazine all the time. A company is serving customers best, for example, by using a particular process or structure, then the customer changes, the product changes, or the competition changes and the people don't notice because they weren't trained to serve the customer, they were trained to be part of the process."

"This 'life of its own' thing is really big," I said, stretching out the last words and drawing both arms up in a big circle around my head.

Just then, we floated into a small rapid, really more of a ripple, which nevertheless rocked the boat and caused me to sit up and wedge my bare feet into the folds of the floor to stabilize myself. Just to the left, the other boats headed for a small sandbar on the bank, where we beached for lunch.

The sand area was no more than fifteen feet across, from river to a rock face that jutted about thirty feet above river level, so the guides had minimum space to set up the lunch table. They moved like a well-oiled machine, unpacking, setting up, and getting ready to spread out the food.

Devin showed Pat a path up through the rock face that led to a natural hot spring. River outfitters, over the years, had carried cement up the steep path and used loose boulders to build a small dam that formed the pool. The edges of the cement were rounded and smoothed by many seasons of sun, wind, and rain.

I stood above the crudely built pool and looked down at the random rocks and oddly placed cement. There was no design, just first come, first serve. If a big rock got there first, it went into the wall. If a bag of cement came next, it got poured. Random and crude, haphazard and loose, it was a perfect pool for part-time river rats like us. We were high enough to see several bends in the river from our morning run, and every section we could see was tainted with brownish, murky runoff from the heavy rain.

I jumped from rock to rock until I was in front of the

pool and had nowhere to go but in, slowly immersing a foot, an ankle, a leg, then two legs. Then—voila, the hot water was tickling the bottom of my chin.

The others followed, and the pool almost felt crowded when Jordan's head peeked over the rock's edge from the trail below.

"Get a move on it," Simon blurted in Jordan's direction. "This hot water may run out soon."

Of course, the hot spring was like the river. It was there before we existed, and it would be there after we were gone. Simon liked to be a cutup, and I could tell he was feeling very gracious toward Jordan for her help on the river. He loved the adventure of this sport, but it looked like his river skills were not as robust as his enthusiasm. Jordan was humble and didn't appear to need acknowledgement or even thanks.

She grinned at Simon's remarks and offered a short reply I didn't hear. Reaching the top of the trail, she stopped for a breath after the steep climb, turned away from us toward the river and looked up the canyon for a moment at our morning traverse and winding descent. Kyle and Pat were comparing personal notes on their river skills that helped them conquer the rapids while Simon studied the dam construction.

Jordan stood atop the rock face, where she slowly

pulled her river shirt up over her head. The skin on her tanned waist and back were cloaked only by a thin bikini strap. She let the shirt fall to the rock at her feet and carefully unbuttoned her shorts. With a wiggle, her shorts dropped to her feet.

Light broke through the battered branches of an old tree overhead, filtering the sun's glare. The small of her back formed a delicate line down to her narrow waist, which gave way to a bikini bottom. While Kyle and Simon talked about the rapids, my eyes remained on Jordan. The uneven sunlight gave her sandy hair a curious tint of reddish-orange as she lowered her body toward her rock perch. The low rumble of the river was the only sound I could hear, and Jordan was the only thing I could see.

"Okay, let's eat it before the flies do," Devin yelled up from the sandy beach below.

Kyle and Simon lined up first for lunch, each piling a paper plate high with sliced ham, turkey, Swiss cheese, tomatoes, and pickles. It takes more fuel to paddle the rapids than to sit at a desk, and my plate was piled high with the same mound of calories as the rest.

I found a semi-flat rock to sit on near Pat and set my root beer next to me on the sand. As the plates emptied, Simon started to chat about his trip to Alaska. I looked up to see the bank across the river, which was a five-foot wall of rock. The light gray limestone face was adorned with stripes of faded iron-red sheets horizontally layered into the rock face. As the riverbed turned sharply left, the water slammed straight into that bank, stripping it of any loose dirt or standing stones. The current bounced off this ribbon of rock and, in fizzling fury, redirected itself down the center of the channel.

"No, we didn't want to take a cruise," Simon was saying. "We wanted to explore the interior and get a feel for the lifestyle. Just take a look at what people do in that part of the world."

"So you got off the coast and into the backcountry? Did you see any drilling rigs?" Kyle asked.

"Not that I recall, and not that much backcountry, really. We did take a two-hour plane ride over the tundra and backcountry, but I'm telling you, that single-engine plane scared my wife to death. We hit a thermal pocket on our way back to the Sitka airport, and it felt like the whole plane dropped forty feet. The pilot just chuckled and said it happens almost every time he's up. But, man, it was scary."

"I'm a senior advisor to an organization that is desperately trying to keep drilling out of the Alaskan wilderness," Kyle said matter-of-factly. "But it will be an uphill battle with the pressure from the big oil companies and the mood Washington is in for more oil at any cost to the environment."

Simon looked up from his plate and nodded in a respectful manner to acknowledge that he was listening.

Kyle continued, "The pristine wilderness has to be preserved for future generations. We've got to make it happen."

Simon's eyes panned the river canyon. Small, calm ripples lapped onto the sandy bank a few feet away. The canyon walls narrowed and disappeared as they wound through the valleys, channeling the river north. His eyes still fixed on the river, Simon opened his mouth and slowly spoke.

"It is really beautiful land." He paused. "The inter-action of the ecology of an area like that, or the entire planet for that matter, is just beginning to be under-stood. I would guess that a hundred years from now we will know a great deal more about the interaction of all species and how they are interdependent. What is that thing about a butterfly flapping its wings in China and affecting the weather in California?"

"It's something like that," Kyle said. "It's from a concept called chaos theory, built on the idea that things are interconnected and many patterns are similar in nature, though the time frame or size may be different."

Pat chimed in, "Simon, here's an example from my business. I can show you two stock charts that look very similar. The ups and downs are in the same places. The lengths of the troughs are just alike, yet one is from a stock's one-year price history and the other is from the last ten minutes of trading."

"But they look the same?" Simon asked.

"Yes, they call it a fractal," Pat said. "A big takeaway here is that things that may seem chaotic or random may be very ordered and have a structure that can only be recognized from a proper vantage point."

"Patty boy, you are turning into a real philosopher. First it's the Zen of fishing and now chaos theory and world order," I said. "Will you be my guru?"

That got a laugh from everybody, even Pat. I looked right at him to bask in my successful dig, and he brought his right hand up to his grinning cheek, extended his middle finger, and began lightly scratching his nose. I couldn't help breaking into a huge grin. Yes, we were out on the river acting like school-boys. The third day was the charm, and the buzz of civilization was out of my head.

Let's go for more, I thought.

"But, Kyle, are environmentalists against driving cars or having electric lights?" Simon asked, breaking off the revelry.

"Don't be silly. Energy production just needs to be accomplished without harming the environment."

"Whose environment?" Jordan interjected. "Maybe it's a bit chauvinistic to protect our pristine lands as long as some foreigners in some far-off place keep drilling and pumping the oil to run our turbines. What if there is a spill there? Who cares, right?"

"Of course we care. Ecology is a worldwide proposition," Kyle replied.

"Well, where is the manual on that?" Jordan said. "Where are the journal articles to protect the pristine wilderness of Saudi Arabia? If you want fossil fuels, you have to drill and pump them. Yes, you have to pump it as cleanly as you can, but you have to take the responsibility to produce it."

Kyle sighed. "Look, little lady, these wilderness lands support many critical species, and if they are destroyed, it erodes our ecological balance. It is crucial that we do all we can to protect them. There are hundreds of species lost every year already."

"Well, how many species are there in the world?" I asked.

"Nobody really knows at this point," Kyle answered.

"If you don't know how many species there are in the world, year to year, how do you know if more are being lost than created or discovered?" I asked. "There's no constant to measure the numbers against."

"There was a loose theory that more species were lost because of pollution and environmental problems," Jordan said, "but the press and the environmental movement successfully changed it to a fact somewhere along the way. A 'known' fact by the general public that has no basis in actual evidence. Nice job, right, Kyle?"

"Some of these things get a little ahead of themselves, but Simon gets it," Kyle said, somewhat hotly. "Even though we know little about the interaction of all species, our long-term survival may depend on it."

"Wouldn't you agree with that, Jordan?" Simon asked.

"I agree wholeheartedly, but what is with the hyperbole and deception?" Jordan said. "Why can't everybody just use the real facts and let's get the job done? Like energy policy. Somebody gets in front of the cameras and says we need an energy policy and the next day the environmental hype- artists are calling him a lunatic and enemy of the people."

"Look, there is oil all over the world yet to be discovered. Let's leave Alaska alone," Kyle said.

I would have rather left this conversation to the rest of the group and taken a walk, but the riverbank was vertical on either side of our beach. I had nowhere to walk except back up the hill to the hot spring, so I stayed. I was getting to feel like my "old civilized self," but clearly, they were already feeling like their same-old-civilized-selves. The three-day rule might be a four-day rule for some in this group, but I was sure they would talk themselves out soon and settle into the beauty of the wilderness.

"Hey, Kyle, how does this whole energy production issue relate to global warming?" I asked.

Simon was looking out at the river and Pat was staring at his lunch, but nobody left the group. It was like watching the local six o'clock news. You really didn't want to watch it, but you couldn't turn it off for fear of missing something juicy. I could feel the silent tension as everybody waited for Kyle's response. He did not disappoint them.

"In a nutshell, carbon dioxide emissions are at such levels that they are overwhelming the atmosphere and triggering a variety of responses that will likely lead to a rapid warming."

"But these kinds of changes take a long time. This is a big planet," Jordan said. "Come on, Kyle, maybe some places are warming, but don't go rabid on us. Some places are cooling."

"Well, there is more carbon in the atmosphere than ever recorded in history, and high carbon dioxide levels are always present during periods of higher global temperatures," he said.

"Nice try, but 70,000 years ago, north America was mostly covered in ice," she replied. "The Great Lakes were scooped out by glaciers," she added. "And there have been other times when the earth had no polar ice caps and it was green everywhere."

Kyle was getting more agitated, and Jordan was circling him like a gnat on a hot summer day. As usual, she was bold and knew some details, but nobody else had the facts to outright dispute him. I was always skeptical of the so-called experts because they often have a dog in the fight, a point to prove. But what was wrong with reducing carbon emissions even if it turns out it's not causing global warming? It is causing air pollution. China is belching so much smoke that people have to wear face masks around some cities. The big picture is that the world is reaching the end of the first industrial revolution, where the standard of living skyrockets because of industrialization, which rose on the back of machines that burn fossil fuels and pour smoke into the air. Maybe the second industrial revolution will bring different kinds of machines and fuels, I thought.

There was a moment of silence as Kyle tried to regain composure. He was pacing in a small circle, his hands clasped together while his face blushed red. He was high- strung and packed full of details on this warming topic, and wasn't tolerating opposition well.

"I don't want to get too technical, especially for Jordan's sake," Kyle snapped.

That got a chuckle from Simon. It would have from me, too, except that I was nurturing my infatuation with Jordan and held it back.

"There are these things known as feedback loops. They are self-feeding cycles that can accentuate a situation like a warming trend," Kyle said. "For example, as the ice melts, the hundreds of square miles of white surface that was reflecting light away is now a darker sea or land that absorbs light, turning it into heat, and this speeds up the warming. There are computer models for these feedbacks, but it is hard to know exactly how these loops function." "Then how do you know these feedback loops will do what the computer models project?" Jordan asked.

"We know they work 'cause we can see them in action," he said. "Look at the force of the last hurricanes to hit the Gulf of Mexico. Conditions are becoming ripe for extreme weather patterns."

"Here you go again," Jordan shot back. "A couple of big hurricanes don't prove the t-h-e-o-r-y of global warm-ing." She elongated the word "theory" for emphasis. The media took the worst-case computer models, the ones scientists never imagined to be plausible, and created their movement."

Kyle's face was red, and I could almost feel the blood starting to boil in his veins. When Devin gave the order to man the boats and get back on the river, Kyle walked over to the trash can and slammed his paper plate into the plastic bucket, keeping his gaze fixed on the sand as he strode to the river's edge. I thought he was holding his own in these spats, but he appeared to be taking the battle a bit too personally. He'll shake it off, I thought.

9

Jordan wadded up her napkin, folded it inside her paper plate, slowly rose from the rock, and walked over to the lunch table. After tossing the paper into the five-gallon plastic trash bucket, she turned and dashed toward the water where Devin stood.

He was facing the river and didn't see her flying toward him. Jordan's arms straightened in front of her, and when she reached Devin she lowered her shoulder and threw her weight into her assault. With just enough force to lift him from his feet, her forward momentum thrust him toward the wide, slow river current. As he crashed into the water, he turned to see Jordan and the look of fear on his face turned to a wide grin. The momentum of Jordan's attack unbalanced her, as well, and she fell toward the water. Devin twisted forward just enough to wrap his arms around Jordan. Just before they both disappeared into the water, he yelled with exuberant glee, "You're comin' in too!"

After a moment, they popped up and swam the few strokes it took to get to knee-high water. To the cheers of everyone on the bank, they turned to each other, locked arms, and stepped onto the dry sand.

He took her right hand and raised her arm into the air like a prizefighter. "The winner," he declared.

We roared with approval, except for Kyle, who was still pacing and red-faced. I clapped with little enthusiasm, because the sinking feeling in my stomach was moving into my throat at the sight of Jordan and the young buck. My thoughts digressed to a time when I was young and full of youthful exuberance. Karen and I used to go to Stinson Beach, north of San Francisco, on Sundays before the kids were born. It was too cold to swim, and sometimes the fog made it almost too frigid to be there at all, but the salt air, and knocking around the tide pools, brought us out again and again. It was free to goof around out there, and we didn't have any money for recreation back then.

One afternoon, an artist friend of hers came with us. We were walking near the water, letting the waves lap on our bare feet when he pulled three soft balls out of his jacket and started nonchalantly tossing them up and juggling them. I thought that was the coolest thing I had ever seen. In a matter of ten minutes, he taught me to rotate those three balls in midair. That week, I bought my own juggling balls and worked on my technique, tried it at parties, but never got as good as I wanted to be. What a quirky little thing to do. I hadn't thought of juggling in years.

There was a small crowd around Jordan and Devin as the action was recounted, blow by blow—the look on Devin's face, the element of surprise, the slap when they hit the water. What was I thinking? I couldn't have a crush on a thirty-four-year-old, I said to myself. What would the kids say? And, what did I need a crush for? I was doing just fine.

10

The first half mile after lunch was a leisurely float. I pulled up next to Devin, and we began talking about the trip and the river.

"What's coming up this afternoon?" I asked.

"A couple of Class 3s," he said, "but the water is unusually high and the obstacles may have changed since last week. It's normal throughout the summer, though. First part of June, when the water is high, a bunch of these fun curls are covered by high water, and by this time of year a lot of the big boulders poke up and the river gets what we call 'more technical'—more holes to run and more rocks to hit your head on. That storm in Montana may be catching up to us. When the water is high, this next rapid can run a little too fast for some people."

"Hey, everybody is loosened up by now. We'll all be okay," I assured him. "That storm looks like it's passed through and gone, anyway."

"Flash floods occur six to eight hours after the storm," he said quietly. "Stay close to Kyle for the next two runs. I'll ask Pat to stay with Simon. Chili for dinner tonight."

"You think those guys are a problem?" I asked.

"Well, not a problem, but Simon is a bit top-heavy and tipsy, and I'm afraid he's losing a little confidence. You need to be loose and agile to float into some of these boogers. Loose hips saves ships, they say."

"I never heard that one," I said. After a pause, I added, "You think Kyle is all right?"

"He's got the skills and the poise to run this river, but he is anything but loose. Keep it to yourself, but Kyle is a danger out here right now. He's getting snappy and combative, and he's getting a little testy about listening to directions—all a bad combination."

"We're going to be okay, right?" I asked.

"I've run it like this in the spring, but not with guests.

If everything goes just right, we'll be fine."

• • •

"Nice move on Devin." Simon floated in voice range of Jordan's kayak. "You probably haven't seen the last of him on this, but he can take defeat like a real man. By the way, I've been overhearing some of your discussions with Kyle, and I agree with a lot of what you're saying."

"Yeah," she said. "There are a lot of big-picture areas that politicians reduce to sound bites. The long-term challenge of managing a complex economy gets diminished to oppositional bickering. But decisions affect people up and down the economic ladder for many years after they're made."

Simon paused, and both he and Jordan paddled along in the calm river current without a word.

Simon pointed to the right with his paddle. "Look over on the bank."

At the water's edge, a small black bear meandered under the partial cover of some scruffy-looking trees. The furry creature glanced up at the kayaks, unfazed, its front paws sinking in the soft mud as it lapped up a drink.

"I love this trip," Simon said quietly.

Jordan nodded and dipped her paddle into the soft water flow—right, left, and right again. Simon stayed beside her, a few feet to her left, and for a moment the river was all there was. We all floated quietly for a long time. After a while, the river widened and the banks receded. The current carried us down the middle of this wider channel, directly into the afternoon sun.

"I've been thinking about this global warming thing," Simon said. "I read that an average American family is said to produce fifty tons of carbon dioxide every year— including their share of the electric grid and commercial trucking and shipping, and so on."

"Yeah, well, this 'attributing' thing is extremely soft data, and much of it is just serving their cause." Jordan paused. "But, all in all, this carbon thing needs to be solved, I guess. I just hate it when these self-serving zealots regurgitate these phony numbers and browbeat the public."

"You may have to get over yourself on this warming thing," Simon said in his fatherly tone.

"Yeah, I know," she replied.

Simon's boat floated into a crosscurrent that pulled him toward the right bank. He paddled forward and worked his way back to the middle of the river where Jordan was quietly paddling downstream. As he joined her, the sounds of the wilderness were all that could be heard, orchestrating its slow, smooth concerto.

Jordan broke the silence. "I hated to leave Alicia at

home when she was the one who invited me. I think she'll be all right, don't you?"

"She took a hard fall, but everything will heal with time. Who would have thought of tennis as a contact sport, anyway?" Simon quipped. "I was a little surprised that you decided to come along anyway. I mean, you didn't know anybody but me, and we're just a bunch of old guys."

"Yeah, well, I had blocked it out on the calendar, and news is a little slow right now, so this is an easy time to get away."

"No romantic, island getaways for you these days?" "Romance left the building along with Elvis, I'm afraid," she replied. "Where did it go?"

"I don't know—maybe he got tired of talking about politics? A great guy, but I suppose we are different kinds of people. What's a girl gonna do?"

"Relationships only work with compromise on both sides, and there has to be commitment, like an ultimate goal both people can strive for. Early on, my marriage suffered from having no goal, just two people doing their own thing at the same time. When Alicia was born, we had an instant long-term focus. All the rest of it faded away, and life settled into a groove. We were a unit, finally. Kids aren't the only way to do it—sports, religion, or politics, they all can work."

"I have this fast-paced-tear-it-up lifestyle, and so did he," she said.

"Maybe you need somebody older?" Simon said. "Or younger," she said.

"A boy toy?"

"An intriguing idea," she said with a giggle.

Simon raised his right hand and pointed to a spot high on the bank. "An eagle's nest on top of that tree," he said softly.

I was in earshot of them talking and looked up just in time to see a bald eagle spread its wings and descend to its perch atop the tallest tree on the bank. We watched in silence as the eagle settled in, and finally Jordan looked at Simon.

"I always say that I don't suffer fools well," she said. "It's kind of an edgy stance to be in all the time."

"You could soften the edges a little and still be the same person you are," Simon replied.

They floated quietly, as if the river were speaking and they were memorizing its every word. The shallow ripples chattered while the deep water groaned, and all of it uttered a quiet truth.

"Yeah," she said. "Probably a little too edgy."

11

I reached the group of kayaks just before Jordan and Simon as Devin began to give his instructions on the rapid coming up.

"I walked up and took a look at this one. It's a new run today because the high water has covered some of the old holes, but it's brought in a few bugaboos on the right and one of the rocks we never worry about is going to be a do- not-go-there spot, so listen up. Run the first wave straight down the middle. After that, your boat will want to move to the right into the big eddy, so after you break through the wave, paddle hard on the right and point your bow toward the left bank. That will set you up for the big hole that is next. Once you are through that, eddy-out on the left and wait for everybody to assemble. Remember"—he raised his voice for emphasis—"do not get caught in the eddy on the right. If you do, don't go down. Paddle upstream, stay in the eddy, and wait for a guide."

"What's the big deal about the eddy?" Kyle blurted. "The eddy is fine, but you do not want to run the right side of the river today, and that eddy will spin you into a huge plume of white water and drop you down onto the jagged boulders below it. We don't want to have to scrape you off those rocks. The water is a little higher than I like to run it with guests, so stay focused." His voice was calm but stern, and he looked directly at Kyle.

The bow of Devin's kayak nose-dived into the hole guarding the first wave and then reversed vertically, shooting up and hitting the water wall perpendicularly. He dug his paddle into the swift current in front and pushed forward, back paddling his craft just to the edge of the promised eddy. He waited there, ready to help the rest of us.

Jordan followed, hitting the first wave at a perfect angle. She paddled hard right, as instructed, and, just before the second wave, she dug her blade into the foamy water, causing her boat to jerk left just in time to hit the wave straight on. She easily floated into the designated eddy and waited.

Pat and I watched Kyle hit the first wave with Simon

close behind him. The wave slammed into the left side of his boat, rolling toward the right. Kyle was nearly pitched out, but then, out of pure force of will, he leaned into the wave, leveled his paddle and jabbed it into the curl. His kayak righted itself and the bow punched through the wave. He made it through the rough part but came out shaky and off-balance. As he hit the small ripples below, he pitched and rolled and, in an instant, capsized and separated from his kayak. Both were safe, however, in the quiet swirl of the eddy. Just to the right, I could see Devin begin paddling ferociously upstream, and then I saw Simon dip into the hole.

"Oh, shit!" Pat exclaimed.

The confusion on the water gave way to chaos, and as I floated in the calm water above the rapid, the action seemed to slow while my field of vision widened. I could see the three boats bobbing in and out of sight while the current surged alongside them, and I could feel the panic as Simon collapsed into the crevice, dropping his paddle while his boat was thrust into the swirling forbidden eddy, and he turned a full circle, and then a half circle, and Devin was able to grab the paddle, and he fought the current and got close enough to shovel the paddle to Simon, who did another half turn and floated by Devin while the current took him straight for the white water plume, and when he hit it he was backward, and the thrust doubled the boat over and threw Simon into the fizzling liquid.

"Let's get down there. It looks ugly!" Pat yelled over the muffled roar of the river.

"What?" I said.

"Hey, guy, are you all right?" he asked.

"Uh, I guess. Yeah, let's get down there," I said.

We both shot through the rapid and joined Jordan, whose view of the incident was largely obstructed. Kyle was near shore, pulling himself from the water, still holding his paddle while his boat floated aimlessly about a hundred yards downstream.

"Are you okay?" Pat shouted to Kyle. "Yeah, yeah, I'm okay. Just waterlogged."

"I need Pat over here now, quick, get a move on it!" Devin called from across the river.

The equipment raft, which had followed behind us, cascaded down the rapid, and Devin flagged it frantically. The oarsman back paddled hard on the right and executed a series of wide sweeps with the left oar. The raft swung to the river's edge about fifty yards downstream from Devin. Just beyond the supply raft was a yellow, flat shape, knocking against the shore. It was Simon's kayak, deflated, floating, ruined.

Devin shouted to the guides, "I need a four-inch bandage, and I need it now!"

Then we saw him, his right arm wrapped around Simon's chest in the waist-deep, calm water. With his left hand, Devin pressed his own shirt onto Simon's forehead.

"He made it," I shouted, breathing a sigh of relief. Jordan frowned. "What do you mean 'made it'?"

"Simon got tripped up and got sucked into those rocks," I answered.

"It wasn't my fault," Kyle said from his tenuous perch on the steep, rugged shoreline. "I slowed up a little just before the hole, just wanted to get a better look at it. Simon was too close. He should have slowed up too, looked at it better. Look, don't blame me."

Kyle looked shaken and worn out. His hair draped down wet and straight, covering both ears, his back hunched slightly just below his shoulders. Jordan shot a perplexed glance at me, and I knew what she was communicating.

"There was nothing you could have done," I said, trying to appease Kyle. "I have seen a lot of wrecks on the river. They just happen and you go on. He'll be fine. The guides know how to handle this."

"Stay put," Jordan shouted. "I'll paddle down and get your boat. Everything's cool." She pointed her bow downstream toward the empty kayak.

Devin dropped his right knee onto the air-filled pontoon of the equipment raft while he bent over to grab Simon's arm. The other guides helped lift Simon into the raft. The water was waist high, and the river bank was at a sharp enough angle to keep the rest of us in our boats.

Simon settled into the makeshift seat the guides made for him on the raft. He was conscious, but looked dazed and groggy. Devin slowly removed his shirt from Simon's forehead, replacing it with a surgical four-inch bandage.

"Okay, let's get everybody over here," Devin said to the group of kayaks assembled around the big raft. "We're alright, and we're going to be just fine. Simon got a nasty gash on his forehead and looks like he has a concussion, but no bones are broken, so there you are. The river is running pretty high, and the next stretch is going to be a little testy. If you go out, remember to let go of your paddle and go down the river feet first to push off the rocks. We will pick you up as soon as possible. Just stay calm."

"Simon needs medical attention. We need to get back to civilization. It's clear we need to get off the river," Kyle snapped. He was looking up and down the river as he spoke, a bit of terror in his eyes.

"No place to get off," Devin countered. "We're in a stretch that is not accessible by any roads. The next eight miles we're on our own. Let's stay focused on the river, and we'll be in front of a fireplace sipping single malt sooner than you think."

"That man needs a doctor—Jesus Christ, Devin, call in a helicopter," Kyle demanded with high-pitched urgency.

"Yeah, well...no place to land, professor." Devin's tone was soft but firm. "The river dug this gulley out over a couple million years, and it's deep and narrow. No, it's eight miles down the river to an armchair and a whiskey, boys and girls. The river's rising 'cause of the rains, but I don't think we'll get any flash flooding. We'll know more when we get to the Middle Fork."

Kyle crossed his arms. "What do you mean? I'm sick of the hocus-pocus. What will the Middle Fork tell us?"

"About six miles down, the middle fork joins the

main fork. The headwaters of the middle are a lot closer to the runoff source, and its canyon is a lot deeper and narrower. If it's flooding now, the main will be flooding soon, and then we may have to go to higher ground for safety." "What do you mean, 'safe—'"

"Shut the hell up, Kyle," Jordan interrupted. The group fell quiet. "We're doing what Devin says, and we are shutting up. Got it?"

12

We ran the next two rapids with no major problems. I went out at the bottom of the second one, and Jordan was drying out from a spill on the first. The clouds parted and the sun was high overhead, warming us up quickly. I pulled out my plastic wraparound sunglasses and flipped the Croaky over the top of my head.

The next three miles had no rapids, but the flat water was running very fast. Yesterday's leisurely paddle strokes were replaced with measured right and left paddling. We stayed in the middle of the flow, settling in single file. The water had risen beyond its usual level, up into the tree line on the steep left bank, as the right bank flattened out, with the rushing water covering the ground in a brown, muddy soup. There wasn't much talking and no river "jabber" or joking or baiting, just floating and waiting.

Simon was behind us on the equipment raft. It was much more stable than the kayaks, and the guides had the experience and know-how to navigate the river. The somber atmosphere carried over to the guides, though, and it was easy to tell that they were treating the river with the respect it deserved.

Devin moved to the right side of the river and found a quiet spot to pull in the frightened troops. As I reached the quiet water of the eddy, I dipped my paddle on the right and pushed forward. The back-paddle motion swung my bow upstream, and I settled in with the flotilla of worn-out vacationers.

Devin addressed the crowd: "Okay, everybody, listen up..."

Floating just behind me, Kyle whispered, "Pat, we've got to get off this river. Simon's hurt, and these guides are amateurs."

"Hey, Kyle, put a cork in it, man. We've got some work to do," Devin shouted over the drone of the river.

Kyle slammed his paddle down on his kayak and looked up, his lips tightly pursed.

Devin continued, "Hey, here's the lay of the land.

Simon had a tough fall and the river is running high, but we can get down this little honey just fine. There is a takeout about four miles or so from here, and the vans will be ready for us. Let's just run it down the middle, and with this flow we can do it in a couple of hours. The good news is that the sun is up and the rain is over, and there is a lodge with showers and the best chili chef in Idaho. Hey, you could have been bored on the beach in Maui. This is adventure! Everybody get to shore and take a break."

The raft pulled in the eddy, its air-filled pontoons bouncing onto the bank. Jordan and I jumped out of our boats and stood waiting for the guide to throw a tie-down rope from the pontoon boat. She waded ankle deep into the water and caught the two-inch nylon rope with both hands as the coil unraveled in midair. She turned and tossed the end to me while holding the curled loop with her left hand. I walked it around a sturdy pine tree and began tying it off, holding the taut line while at the same time moving the end, over and under, tying two half hitches.

Then I felt a warm touch on my hand. I turned and saw Jordan crouching next to me. Her hand stayed on mine, and she gave a slight squeeze. I remember smiling a little. She didn't smile or frown but looked directly at me. Her eyes widened, and I found myself engulfed in her stare.

As she pulled her hand away, she rested her thumb just below my palm, where she began to rub in a circular motion. She looked up at me in silence. Her index finger stroked the taut line of scar tissue that caught her attention. The injury was not visible except for a faint white line of skin at close inspection. Jordan softly massaged the half-inch stripe. Her eyes moved up, but her gaze went right through me.

A few years ago, while playing a pickup game of basketball, a friendly match had suddenly become extremely competitive, as they often do with boys of all ages. Jumping for rebounds off the backboard, three of us tangled our feet in midair, landing our collective weight like a drunken squid on hard, weather-torn asphalt. My knee hit the pitted surface first, opening the skin in a spurt of red blood. My left hand went down and caught the brunt of the fall from the descent of the snarling bodies. The rutted surface and loose gravel left a two-inch gash on my palm. The wound took two months to heal, and the scabs slowly turned to a new layer of soft, white skin rutted in the mirror image of the weather-furrowed asphalt.

"Sports?" she said, half asking, half telling, not expecting a reply.

Then she said, "I'll tie a bowline, it'll hold better."

She tied the mariner's knot with ease around the tree while I stood in silence.

Pat brought over an apple and a granola bar for each of us. Jordan took hers and turned to walk to the raft. Then she stopped, turned back around, and looked at me with a brief glance, hopped on the raft, and began talking to Simon.

"This whole thing is a piece of cake," Pat said after Jordan left. "River is running a little high, but it's like this in the spring, anyway. A little testier, but that's part of the fun. Are you and Jordan getting a little friendly?"

"Naw, she's just helpful when she can be," I answered. I felt light-headed, a slight flutter in my chest. *She's interested?* Maybe, maybe not. Kind of aggressive? Maybe, maybe not. She's a different type of girl. Don't push it, I thought, let things unfold.

I sat down to watch the river and thought about Jim's last two years in Singapore with JP Morgan, and Georgia with two more years at UCLA. Both of my kids had managed to grow up in good shape, and soon nobody would be left in the nest, essentially having left two years ago. I called them both on their cell phones about every week, and I made sure Georgia had enough money for school, but our visits were few and far between.

Raising independent, self-reliant, and most of all self- supporting kids was my goal, but for a while I felt a little abandoned once they were both out of the house. After staying under the radar for a month, Jim would call and pick up the conversation like everything was the same as he'd left it. He thought time stopped for me when he left, that things would always be the same.

The funny thing was, they were much the same. I'd been the single parent for ten years, and that included all of Jim's high school time. I put together a routine that worked for everybody: soccer, theater, homework, and running a company. We all made it through with a certain amount of respect for each other. I had some opportunities with dating, but nobody seemed to fit in with the family, the job or our routine. I could admit to being too picky. There is a certain amount of comfort to just being on your own, too, making up your own schedule, your own friends, not having to small talk or go shopping for cute tops at the boutiques. If I wanted a quiet night, I got it, no questions asked.

Of course, if I didn't want it quiet, sometimes I got it anyway.

13

The trees on the bank were firmly rooted, some in fertile soil while others rested precariously on hard, rock surfaces, sending roots down to wherever they could find a toehold against the harsh rain and wind. But these land-loving old salts on the bank were not accustomed to the current's persistent, high water force. The banks were striped of leaves, twigs and small branches, all of it washed into the relentless flow downstream.

I paddled around several clumps of tangled debris, pushing some of them away from my boat's vulnerable plastic sides. We ran through stretches of rapids that had virtually disappeared because the high water submerged the previously imperiling rocks, converting waves, curls, and holes into flat, fast water. The river did not run easily, though. The swift current could sweep you to either side of the river into logs or branches or newly formed eddies, isolating you from the group, and any mistakes were accentuated by the fast flow.

My heart racing, I could not relax; each paddle stroke was deliberate and measured to keep my craft in the right flow of the river—down the middle, following Devin. I caught up to Pat, who turned his shoulders between strokes, cocked his head slightly and showed his teeth in a wide smile. He saw it all in my face: grim and bleak and way too serious.

"You need to lighten up, buddy," Pat admonished. "It's best to stay loose. You'll do your best staying loose." I looked ahead and saw Kyle and Jordan. Kyle was paddling almost twice as fast as Jordan. The bow of his kayak lurched left then right as his power strokes disoriented his craft. He extended his arms forward with a determination that literally lifted him off the seat. His paddle cut into the murky liquid and his whole body drove the water back. Jordan was saying something delicately to him as her even, unhurried strokes propelled her craft straight and steady down the current.

"Is Kyle okay?" I asked Pat.

"I don't think he is," Pat answered. "He's acting panicky, a little erratic. Jordan is sticking with him through this stretch, just to keep an eye on him."

"That sounds good. Did Devin ask her to do it?" "No, I think she just picked up on the panic back at the last stop and is trying to help," Pat said. "I don't think he's her type, don't worry."

Pat and I rounded a bend and saw the group gathering near the right bank. We arrived and Devin began.

"The middle fork merges just below here, but there is no telling what to expect. So, I want everybody to stay put right here while I walk over that ridge and get a look at it. There is a way through it, but it won't be anything like we're used to."

Kyle blurted, "How hard could it be? Let's just run it. We just need to get off this river. We have an injured person. We're wasting time!"

The group fell silent. Jordan turned her head slightly to the left and looked directly at me. Her eyes widened and rolled. Devin unceremoniously dropped his head, and the only sound was the low rumble of the river.

"It won't take long. This is the right way to do it. I've been running rivers for ten years." He paused. "When the raft gets here, get a snack and fill up your water bottles. I'll be back."

He looked over the group, resting his gaze briefly on Pat, Jordan then me, as if to gauge our states of mind. He took a deep breath, turned, and sprinted up the hill. We beached our boats high on the shore to prevent any sudden current from floating them away and began stretching our legs and aimlessly milling around. The atmosphere was heavy, and when the raft arrived it was a welcome relief to just open the granola bars and replenish our water, all mindless tasks that kept us busy and made the waiting easier.

I walked over to Jordan, and we talked about paddling and the boats and the trash in the water—all small talk. She seemed distracted, and I felt that special connection between us fading away until I noticed she was keeping an eye on Kyle.

"Is he all right?" I asked.

"No, really panicking," she said in almost a whisper.

"The river is pretty tough," I replied. "We're in a small flood situation."

"That's why everybody needs to have their wits about them, and Kyle...well, what can I say?"

I watched Jordan form the words, her lips moving judiciously, precisely. The heat of the afternoon sun felt blistering standing on shore. Jordan pulled her T-shirt off and wrapped it around her waist. The scant bikini top covered little, and I watched a bead of sweat roll from her neck into the soft cleavage of her breasts. She caught my gaze and returned it.

"What's your life about?" she asked. "Who are the people in your life?"

"A son, a daughter and a company—pretty boring, I guess," I replied.

"I'll bet it's not all that boring," she said, then looked to her right and quickly back to me. "Where is he? Where is Kyle? One of the kayaks is gone."

Pat ran to the edge of the water and waded in up to his knees. Facing the glaring afternoon sun, he raised a hand to shade his eyes.

"He's headed downstream," Pat shouted.

Jordan bolted for her boat. With no effort, she leaped into the seat, scooped up her two-bladed paddle and in seconds was in the flow of the river, charging after Kyle. I looked at Pat watching Jordan dart away.

"What's going on?" I practically yelled at Pat.

"Listen, let them go. We wait for Devin and the raft. That's the plan. Stick to the plan. They'll be all right. Jordan will catch up to him and talk him into waiting for us."

I stood on the bank next to Pat, staring into the sun, watching two kayaks turn into specks on the sun- drenched river. Jumping in my kayak, I shouted back at Pat that I needed to catch them. His admonition to hold up before she got to the middle fork was barely audible over the river's growling thunder. I joined the downstream flow of the river, paddling hard for about five minutes until I could see them ahead of me.

They were in the middle of the raging flow, stalled in a large, tranquil eddy formed behind a giant boulder. As I got nearer, I saw Jordan's head jerking back and forth, front to back, her mouth moving quickly. The quiet subtleties in her speech were gone. She was yelling at Kyle, who was shaking his head side to side.

The roar of the current prevented me from hearing either of their voices, but now I could see what Devin had feared the most. The middle fork flowed into our river at a sixty-degree angle, but the calm flow had turned into a torrent. The merging river was swollen over its banks, and the raging water flooded onto the barren shoreline. Where the rivers met, a six-foot wave formed a giant wall of water curling upstream toward us. Rocks and small boulders churned and rotated through this devil's soup. I had never seen anything like it. This was no place for rubber kayaks. The vacation was over. This was true peril.

My boat rushed toward the arguing couple as I hit the fast water just above them. A high white-capped curl threw me to the right. I leaned into the mouth of the wave, shoved my paddle deep into its throat and pulled forward. My boat leveled out and shot through the wave.

I made two hard sweep strokes on my right side to pull into the eddy with Kyle and Jordan, but the current swept me past them.

Landing near a small, shallow rock ledge, I got out of my boat and waded in two feet of water to the dry granite. The shouting appeared to have stopped on the river. I threw my hands into the air, waving them back and forth to get their attention. I motioned them over to me with desperate gestures when Jordan's hand patted the top of her head, the river signal for "okay."

She turned the bow of her boat upstream and caught the flow. With three firm sweep strokes, she directed her boat in a straight trajectory to my rock beach. Kyle seemed to be following Jordan—then his kayak suddenly rotated, sweeping him backward through the bottom of the eddy directly downstream.

The strong current caught the stern and rotated it again, pointing him toward the opposite bank.

Kyle paddled ferociously. Right and left strokes, back strokes, but he could not gain control. He spun several more times, and finally the eddy spit him out into the speeding current. Hitting a small wave backward, the boat's impact almost turned it over. His paddle was jolted from his hands. His reached out grabbing for the floating paddle, but it was whisked away out of his grasp by the foaming white current.

Jordan jumped out of her boat and quickly waded over to shore. We ran to a high point on our rock island and watched as Kyle rode his rudderless craft down to a hapless fate. His boat rotated, hitting a series of ripples bow first. Then the boat slowly spun sideways, and Kyle grabbed both gunnels as he hit the six-foot wall of water.

Debris from upstream churned under the gurgling soup, and as the yellow boat was absorbed by the water, we saw a giant uprooted tree being thrown out of the cauldron onto the surface...right on top of Kyle. Jordan let go a bloodcurdling scream that echoed throughout the canyon. She dropped her face into her palms and started sobbing. I reached over and touched the small of her back. She turned and embraced me with both arms, laying her head on my shoulder.

I held tightly for half a minute as her near-hysteria died down and her body relaxed. As her head rose from my shoulder, she pulled away from my embrace.

"Let's go," she said, and took a step toward our beached kayaks.

"We can't go down there!" I cried. "These little boats can't run that water. Hell, no boat can run that. It would be suicide."

"Come on," she shouted, continuing on down the jagged rock surface to the boats.

I ran after her down to the water, with no intention of either following Kyle into that abyss or allowing Jordan to go.

"Jordan, stop right there. You cannot go down that river. I mean it."

"We're not going down the river. We're going across to the other side. If he's alive, maybe we can fish him out below the choppy water. I think we can walk over that ridge and down to the bank over there. We have to get to the other side."

"Yeah, but there's no way to cross right here. It's too fast. One mistake and we'll join Kyle."

"Look at that eddy on the other side, about thirty yards down," she shouted. "We run the current down the middle, paddle hard right just above that boulder sticking out. Do you see where I mean?"

"Yeah, I see it, but—"

"Paddle hard right there," she said. "The bow should move into the eddy, and as it does, back stroke on the left and the upstream current of the eddy will pull you in. Then just paddle to the bank."

Despite her calmer tone, I thought Jordan had crossed over to hysteria. The best chance for success for that little plan was fifty percent. The other fifty involved certain death.

"Look, slow down," I retorted. "We need to walk these boats up a few hundred yards and cross up there. We can wait for the others."

"There's no time. He still might have a chance. We've got to get—"

This time I cut her off.

"Kyle is dead. He is drowned or crushed or both. You saw that tree come down on top of him, and...that water has thousands of pounds of force. Get a grip!" I was screaming over the roar of the river.

I stood face to face with Jordan as we argued. I was

adamant, and she was cocksure of herself. Neither of us wanted to give ground. It was a matter of life and death for us both. For her, it was Kyle's life. For me, it was our lives. It was my turn in the argument, and I started at her, yelling in her face.

Suddenly her right hand darted behind my neck. She cupped the curve of my neck and pulled my head down level with hers. She rocked forward on her toes, and when her mouth met mine, I felt the tension leave my body. She held her warm lips to mine, and I slowly surrounded her body with each of my arms, one at a time, locking them around her lower back. Our lips parted, and she looked at me for a split second before I kissed her again.

My arms tightened around her, and the soft flesh of her lips melted my resolve to argue. Now we would walk upriver and wait for the others, I thought. It was still going to be a long afternoon. If we found Kyle at all, it would be a terrible sight. We would have to load his body on the raft to take him back, and how was the raft going to get down through this stretch anyway?

"Okay, let's go," she said.

Jordan broke away from our embrace, jumped in her

boat and darted out to the main channel. Without thinking, I followed, paddling ferociously. She pointed her boat downstream, heading for the big rock. About eight feet out, she dug her paddle deep into the swirling water and executed three wide strokes. On the last one, she leaned so far right, I thought the kayak would tip over, but instead the thrust of the paddle heaved the boat to the opposite side and her bow surged into the eddy. A quick back stroke on the left and she settled into the quiet water. I paddled hard toward the rock and started my sweep strokes as instructed. My bow started to turn left, but then I felt the boat lift from the back and undulate forward. A freak wave tossed my boat off its trajectory, head-on into the big rock. The right gunnel scraped against the smooth granite and the force of the water pinned the craft against the rock. The roar of the river was deafening and the spray from the churning water pelted my eyes.

I tried to push off the rock with the blade of my paddle. I had lost sight of anything but the water and my nemesis—the rock—when I felt a small strand lay softly across my shoulder; it was line, attached to a small red- and-white buoy.

I looked over my shoulder and saw Devin on the bank, looping the other end around the only stout tree in sight. I tied the rope to the ring on the front of my kayak and started paddling for my life. Devin stood behind the tree and pulled his end of the line. The coils of the rope slid around the tree as he backed up.

As my boat broke away, I made the mistake of leaning away from the rock, into the current. The left gunnel dipped level to the water's surface, allowing a small flow into the craft. Then, in a split second, the gunnel plunged below the waterline under the rushing flow. At the same moment, the boat filled and tilted left. As the kayak made its half turn to upside down, I felt myself gently being laid into the cold, brown, liquid fury. The bright, glaring afternoon sun turned black as the boat flipped over my bobbing head and shoulders. I let go of my paddle and grabbed a taught cord inside the boat, my knees grazing and bouncing off the submerged rock as my boat and I joined the downward flow.

The standard-issue life vest kept my head upright, but the spray and churning of the water splashed into my eyes and mouth, wiping away any feelings of safety. Fear piled on like a three-hundred-pound line-backer. My legs dangled in the deep current and I managed to pull them together in a halfhearted scissor-kick while pushing on the upriver side of the kayak. A sliver of light peeked through the gap as the boat tossed on the surface, but the kayak would not right itself.

All outside sound was muffled, and I was stuck following Kyle into certain death. What seemed like a lifetime was only a few seconds, while the river veteran, Devin, held tight to my lifeline and reeled me toward the shore into the safety of a swirling eddy. When my feet touched the river bottom, I stood, raised both arms and tossed the boat over my head to the side.

Standing there like a cold, wet rat, I shouted at Devin on the shore, "Did you see Kyle?"

"Yeah, I saw Kyle, but I also saw you," he replied. "What kind of trick was that? You have a death wish?"

"Christ!" I said almost under my breath. "It's a long story."

A few minutes passed by in silence as Devin pulled the kayak to land, and I waded to the shoreline and sat down. Fear and confusion took over my body, and I stared at the river but only saw white space in front of my eyes. My mind went blank.

"I saw Kyle go in, didn't see him come out," he said. "It's pretty bad. Walk up to the others and tell them to bring the raft down here and wait for me. I'm going downstream to look for him."

"I'm going with you," Jordan said, appearing from around a giant boulder.

Devin paused, looking at Jordan then back at me. After a few long seconds, he said, "Okay, let's all go."

14

Just a few days before, when the twin-engine Air Idaho plane dropped into the town of Salmon, I couldn't have foreseen the turmoil ahead. From the air, the snow on the rugged mountains looked like a patchwork of white and brown. The raw rock peaks were windswept and, from five thousand feet, breathtaking.

My mind digressed to a similarly spectacular view of the Rocky Mountains from a Boeing 747, at thirty thousand feet. The view from there is like watching a nature video in the comfort of your own den. But from a fraction of that altitude, those white, craggy peaks in Idaho were more real, and more ominous, as if subtly issuing their own warning about the dangers in their midst.

We were in a disaster situation, and Kyle could be dead. Survival was the only mandate. My mind wandered, and I had trouble staying focused on where we were and what we were doing. I guess I wasn't sure what we had to do, who was doing it, or what would happen next. I was in shock, or something like it. My mind seemed to flash second by second on a thousand things. Then the last few days on the river stuck in my thoughts: white water, fishing, business, kids, and Muffin. I was used to controlling my surroundings; running a business, that's what you have to do. But no one could control this river and this flood.

I struggled to keep up with Devin and Jordan. Their eyes were straight ahead, fixed on their task. Slightly dizzy, I felt like sitting down. Beads of sweat rolled down my chest and my thoughts kept rambling.

The world seemed to go into slow motion. The sounds of the river dulled, then vanished altogether. The light flashes gave way to a flat glow. My mind raced on, frantic to think this thing through and solve it— right now. I didn't have the wherewithal to wonder why.

I lifted my leg to step over a large rock, and my right knee gave way under my own weight, almost throwing me to the ground. The sun flashed in my eyes.

Jordan glanced back over her shoulder as she stepped to the top of a small granite formation. She turned to face me.

"You're white as a sheet. Sit down right now," she demanded.

Devin stopped and turned but did not say a word.

They both walked back to me and sat down.

"I can't seem to focus," I said, "and I'm feeling a little faint."

Devin handed me a bottle of water. Nobody spoke. The emotional exhaustion had caught up with all of us, and the weight of our predicament was just now fully sinking in. Jordan wedged herself in between two rocks and rested her back on a third while Devin sat stoically, back straight, his gaze straight ahead. My eyes closed, and I dozed off for a few minutes while sitting straight up.

I woke up to Devin's gentle voice, "Jackson, how are you feeling? We need to cover some ground. If we are going to find him, we need to do it now."

My eyes opened slowly, but right away I could tell the nap worked miracles. I felt more focused, and the dizziness had passed.

15

We followed Devin over a steep rock mound, across a gray granite ledge, and down to the riverbank. I scanned the area for any sign of Kyle or his kayak, but saw nothing. Jordan waded to a giant boulder just offshore, climbed to the top and surveyed the swollen riverbanks downstream. Nothing.

"What are we going to do?" Jordan asked.

"I'm not leaving anybody down here, and that's final," Devin said, with a solid resolve back in his voice. "We'll find him. You guys walk upstream and look on both sides. I'm going down around that bend. Here, blow this whistle if you find something."

He handed me a silver whistle tied to a loop of old cotton string, then turned and trotted downriver through the trees. I opened my hand and looked at the whistle. A bolt of sunshine reflected from the chrome surface, causing me to squint. I raised it to my lips and took a breath, ready to blast it.

Jordan had taken a few steps along the bank and was looking upstream, scanning for clues to Kyle's whereabouts. I looked down at the whistle, and without blowing it, slipped it into my pants pocket. She and I walked for a few minutes and then she stopped, turned toward me and took my hand. Her rosy cheeks had turned pale, and she looked like a changed person.

"Look, things are tense and there's a lot of anxiety out here and sometimes people do things they wouldn't normally do. I understand that, and I want you to know that if you want to forget our little smooch up there, it's okay with me. I'll understand."

"You really meant it then?" I asked.

"Well, yeah. I don't go around kissing random boys, at least not too often."

"I'm not exactly a boy anymore."

I pulled her closer and kissed her. She put her arms around my back and her body pressed against mine. We took a breath and kissed again. Whatever this turned out to be in the long run was irrelevant right now. I liked this intimacy with Jordan, but we were both shaky and needed assurance. I thought it was all probably temporary. Just deal with the panic and fear now, I thought, and keep it light.

"You know," I said. "I'm kind of a square and I have grown kids and I don't live in L.A. Is this a one-river stand for you?" I hoped she would go along with this mood change.

"We can make it what we want. I know what I want." We stood locked in an embrace, and I kissed her again.

Her soft lips parted slightly, and the faint hint of her warm breath sent a shiver down to my toes.

Jordan and I fanned out along the riverbank, which was thick with debris caught in bushes and small trees that normally were high above the waterline that time of year. I hoped the red paddle jacket would give away Kyle's location.

Pulling up logs and limbs, I looked in pools and under bushes, but found no trace. Finally, I stopped while balancing on two rounded boulders, the soles of my treaded river shoes clinging to the polished granite. I looked upstream in frustration. That's when I saw the red fabric shredded in long, narrow, uneven strips clinging to a brush-covered limb.

I made my way along the steep bank, dipping into the water when the land receded into a sharp vertical wall, eliminating my walking path.

About thirty yards up, I found Kyle's jacket—or what was left of it.

I looked up, my eyes scanning for any possible new clues. I saw nothing that would lead me to our lost colleague. Five wild geese swept in formation down into the canyon. They hovered, gliding in midair, then dove together just a few feet from the water's surface, wings fixed, into the headwind of a downstream air current. I stood fixated on their flight, watching the small flock round the bend in the canyon. My gaze left the birds and followed a line of sight into the heavily wooded slope beyond the river.

As if directed by a grand conductor, the birds all banked right, still hovering what looked to be only inches from the surface before disappearing from sight.

Just then I heard the muffled shriek of a police whistle and darted toward the sound. When I caught up with Jordan, we painstakingly worked our way down a stretch of shoreline, following the whistle, until we found Devin, leaning over a clump of bushes by a newly formed pool of brown water. He had broken and bent the thin twigs and was standing knee-deep in the pool. Kyle was lying on one side, wedged among a random tangle of small branches, his legs twisted and bent just below the waist in a contorted, unnatural way. A ripped, tattered shirt clung to his body, its gaping holes revealing his pale, sallow skin. "He's still breathing, but looks pretty broken up," Devin said. "It's going to take all three of us to get him to dry land. Jordan, pick up his legs just under his knees. I'll support his back. Okay, lift."

Kyle made no sound or movement. We laid him in the leaves on his back. His right shoulder was cinched up near his ear, and it looked like the collar bone was broken. A knee was turned sideways and twisted, and his lower leg dangled at an odd angle. No sign of major bleeding, though, at least on the surface. He was breathing evenly.

"Kyle, can you hear me?" Jordan blurted, but he made no sound. "Kyle?"

"I've got to get the raft down here." Devin sounded out of breath. "The splints and medical gear are mandatory now, and the satellite phone is there. The helicopter can pick him up about a half-mile down at a burnout from the fire in ninety-one. I'm not letting anybody die on my trip."

"How does the raft make it through the river from up there?" Jordan demanded.

"I have a few tricks up my sleeve. I'll bring it down. I told you, everybody gets out while I'm in charge."

Devin took off in a sprint. Like a wild young buck, he darted through the trees, around the rocks and disappeared. Jordan hovered over Kyle, propping his head up and clearing the brush from around him. Then she sat down beside me and pulled her knees up to her chest. I laid my arm around her waist. She dropped her head on

my shoulder and began to sob. I tightened my hold, and she inched closer.

"Things turned bad so quick," Jordan confided. "We went from a vacation to disaster in a matter of hours. Kyle is a nice person. I can't imagine him in this situation."

"I feel the same way. You guys have different opinions on things."

"Yeah, it's good-natured debate. I get a little worked up sometimes, but I thought he handled himself okay. But, really, I can't even think about it now. I just don't know about anything."

She exhaled with those words, as if all the breath left her lungs and, with it, all her energy and resolve. There was a long silence before she said, "Anyway, I don't take it personally. It's ideas, not people. Kyle is part of our group. He needs us now."

The only sound was the roar of the river for a long time while we caught our breath and thought about our situation. I wanted to say something, anything, but nothing found its way past my lips. Kyle was our biggest worry, but if he and Simon could get busted up, so could any of us.

The finality of being on our own without help was a dire thought. Jordan was reaching a stress point. I knew I had to buck up and stay steady—nerves of steel. When Karen died, I felt like everything was caving in around me. I had been working ten-hour days to make the business successful. I had to—well, at least I thought I did—and the kids were way too young for the trauma of losing their mother. I pulled myself together and got them through it and back on track. Standing tall in the hurricane—that was me, no prob-lem. Well, the hens came home to roost a year later, the trauma of it all crept in. I would go to bed exhausted, only to wake up in an hour buzzing like a bee. I'd break out in a cold sweat at work, shaking like a leaf. It was like battle trauma, my doctor said—post-traumatic stress.

Over the years I recovered, but right now it was a battle again. I needed a strong game face. I had trained myself to lead in business. This was a different setting and Devin was in charge, but I wanted to be ready to be a strong player.

Time was ticking by, and none of the crew showed up.

Again, I felt the need to say something, to get some conversation going, to get our minds off the waiting. I wanted to think of a way to lighten things up.

"So, okay, just between you and me," I finally said, "who are you, Miss Jordan? I mean, where did you come from? Just what makes you tick like a precision Swiss watch, anyway?"

"Tick-tok around the clock," she answered, deflecting my question.

"Come on, help me out here, tell me about Jordan." The Swiss watch was beginning to miss a few beats, but I didn't bring that up. She didn't say a word, and the air between us started to thicken and crust over like a bowl of old pea soup. I was pushing, and she was in no mood to chitchat. After a long minute of silence, she spoke.

"I want to tell you a children's story that my father

used to tell me. I always thought he made it up because it's a little perverse, but I kind of like it anyway."

"Okay," I said with trepidation, and some measure of anticipation.

"It goes like this: Montrose de la Mouse was the oldest descendent of the original clan founders. The clan dominated the East Kingdom for over twenty generations. The kingdom was comprised of a half-acre corner in a fallow cow pasture on a hillside in the south of France, a few miles north of Nice near the French Riviera. The clan was started by two brothers, Pierre and Boudreaux, who, out to seek their fortunes, came upon a thick, grassy field next to a small thicket of wild strawberries. They stopped for an afternoon meal, and after having eaten all they could eat and stuffed their pockets with all they could carry, walked ahead only to find a patch of lillykiles, the grass with the tasty roots that melt in your mouth just like mother's special jacky-dill fudge. They ate another meal, and by the time their stomachs stopped aching, they realized that there could be no better place to live than right there.

"The clan started small, but grew rapidly along with the underground tunnels and subterranean chateaus for all the clan members. The thick grass in the field gave perfect cover from hawks and catywapuses that might try to sneak around and scoop up a poor, unsuspecting mouse. All the mice worked hard to build storage chambers for strawberries, roots and seeds for the winter, but nobody worked harder than Pierre and Boudreaux. On the weekends, when all the people of the clan were having picnics, three-legged races, and drinking lillykile beer, Pierre would toil alone in his laboratory working on new inventions that would bring a better life for the clan. For example, even though the underground strawberry chambers were stuffed full of the red, delicious fruit each fall, by mid-spring the produce was spoiled and covered in mildew. Pierre finally discovered, through much trial and error, that elmwood oak leaves could be coated with a thick layer of boneybak sap to virtually eliminate the moisture from the wet winter soil. Boudreaux found a way to bend one end of a boneybak thorn to form a hooked end that snugly fastened the leaves to the dirt walls.

"The clan then realized that by the time the summer strawberries were ripe, the stored fruit from last season was still juicy and tasty. So, the next season they began selling stored berries to neighboring clans who were glad to have the winter nourishment. The next few generations of the de la Mouse clan expanded the tunnels and storage capacity so everyone had plenty to eat. Trade and commerce provided enough seeds, roots, juices, and lillykile beer for everyone. After a while, the clan leaders were so busy keeping the accounts and inventories in good order that they stopped doing any of the productive work, like picking the produce or cleaning tunnels. In fact, they had the workers dig deeper and wider burrows for the governing sect of the clan to house the papers and records. They added lounges and sleeping quarters and even racket courts for much-needed recreation, for many of the rulers rarely left the tunnels anymore. Workers were instructed to bring the ripest strawberries, the tastiest seeds, and the best beer to the government offices. Soon, so much of the summer crop was stored and traded away to neighbors that the regular members of the clan had to forage often for extra seeds and berries to survive the winter.

"Your dad sounds like a strange, or let's say unique guy," I said.

"Yes, no doubt about it, but the story is almost over," she said.

"One day, the governors summoned fresh-picked fruit and hot lillykile-root soup for a special celebration. They waited and waited but nobody came with the banquet meal. Finally, Montrose de la Mouse sent his nephew to check on the food, and to everyone's surprise, the tunnels and caverns were empty. Everyone had left and the governors were alone. Montrose, himself, toured the storage chambers and with shock and surprise discovered that each one was totally empty. The governors then proceeded in a group through the tunnels until they emerged into the light of an autumn day.

"An early-winter chill was in the air, the sky was covered with broken clouds, and the strawberry vines were stripped naked of their juicy fruit. The governors filed one by one back into the tunnel and assembled around their large oval table. All was quiet while Montrose tried to conjure up a solution befitting his great ancestors, Pierre and Boudreaux, for the winter was setting in and there was no food to be had. Alas, nothing came to mind, and he wished he had a nice, fresh glass of lillykile beer."

My eyelids felt like a ton of lead, and as soon as Jordan's story ended, I nodded off to sleep.

16

I opened my eyes and stared at the white waves curling into the murky bloated river. The crystal-clear purple and orange waters of two days ago had changed to a brown, almost olive color in the low afternoon sun. The silt-filled soup carried the runoff from hundreds of miles upstream on down to the Snake and Colorado rivers and to the Gulf of Mexico.

Jordan was lying still next to me. I started to turn. "Shh! Don't move," she whispered. "Snake near Kyle's head."

My eyes darted toward Kyle. About two feet from his left ear, a fat, slinking reptile slithered slowly toward the water. We lay still behind its line of sight. The snake stopped, as if sniffing Kyle, moved down next to his shoulders and unhurriedly began to form a coil. I felt

Jordan dart up. She grabbed a two-inch thick branch stripped of its bark by the river, and before I could blink, slammed it down on the coiling intruder.

The snake turned to face Jordan and, without hesitation, struck at Jordan. Her right foot, which had stepped forward for her attack, was in full retreat, and the snake landed on the mushy ground just short of its target. I rolled slowly to my side and quickly crouched on my knees. Jordan was between me and the attacking reptile. I had no idea what I was going to do and categorically had no clue what Jordan thought she was doing. As I rose, a bright burst of light flashed by my eyes. I stopped and looked at the muddy riverbank about five yards away. A small piece of aluminum jutted from the soggy soil—a paddle! In one motion, I jumped to my feet and grabbed the exposed shaft with both hands.

Jordan slowed her withdrawal, stood firmly and waved the stick at the snake, again challenging it. It snapped its long body into a rounded coil, waved its head in Kyle's direction then back to Jordan. Jordan gestured and jeered with the pole, and when she leaned forward with a lunge, the snake again uncoiled and struck. She let out a loud scream and dropped the pole while the snake again slapped the ground, its full length extending like a taut rope.

The aluminum paddle blade severed the reptile's head and its long, cylindrical body undulated violently. Jordan stepped back as I ran to her and grabbed her left forearm, holding it up to look for the wound.

"Missed me," she whispered. "Hit the stick instead."

"But you yelled. I thought you were hit."

"I thought I was, too. It scared the hell out of me. Where did you find that paddle?"

"I saw it buried in the mud, just grabbed it and came up behind him. Glad it worked," I said.

"You're my hero. I'm yours for life."

I knew she was teasing, but when she said it, I felt a twinge in my chest. The subtle humor was a tension release for us both. There was no time for sentimental endings, I thought.

And yet, right now there was nothing but time and waiting. We were waiting for Devin and the crew to get down here with the raft, waiting for Kyle to get hauled out of here, waiting for nightfall, waiting for some food to be cooked, waiting to get off this river, waiting for Kyle to die, maybe, and waiting—at least I was—for Jordan's warm lips on mine again. All this flashed through my mind in a split second. Then my eyes focused again on Jordan.

"Was that bastard going after Kyle?" I asked.

"Hell, I don't know what snakes do. I'm a business major."

I scooped up the severed head with the paddle and hurled it into the current. Jordan started clearing more brush from around Kyle, who didn't move.

"Do you think Devin will make it down soon?" she asked.

"He may have to empty the raft to float it past the middle fork. Maybe the others have to walk over the ridge, I don't know."

"Can Simon make a walk like that?" she asked.

"Well, no broken bones, going slow, they'll get him over. He has to make it, though. Nobody can float that stretch in a rubber kayak."

17

The air was dead calm, and the swollen river flowed past us with a low rumble. A large, round fire pit held a roaring blaze. The branches above quivered in the rising heat. Devin's crew had emptied the supply raft for its run past the bad water. Then they loaded it back up and floated it down to camp.

While Pat and I cooked the chili, Jordan helped make Kyle comfortable. He regained consciousness just before dark and suffered through an awkward process of fitting splints on his shoulder and knee. An ace bandage held them all together, but the slightest movement caused a sharp pain from his shoulder straight down his spine. He became slightly more moveable as the Vicodin and codeine took effect, but I knew tomorrow was going to be tough for him. Still, the mood around camp softened, and people's spirits lightened. There was a bit of joking, and I even saw Jordan's run-and-skip again, around the camp.

Walking over to Kyle's tent, I could hear Devin talking in a low, measured voice. Although I wanted to ask Kyle why he took off like that, Devin was focusing on getting him to safety. Where was the pain? What could he move? How did he feel? Devin was standing tall in the hurricane. He was in charge, and I knew that we were going to do things his way, till we got home, and I was glad about that. Devin had gotten through to the ranger station on the satellite phone. A helicopter was meeting us in the morning, but we had to float Kyle a half mile down a river which showed no signs of calming down. He was complaining about pain in his stomach and lower back, and we feared he had internal damage. This was the deepest part of this ancient gorge, where roads did not exist. From rim to river was a mile deep and rim to rim was at least ten miles across. The flooding had ruled out rescue teams floating down here.

Simon was recovering but still dizzy and needed help getting settled for the night. Back in civilization, he would have been in a hospital being treated for a concussion. He hobbled over the ridge earlier with the help of two guides and now sat with us around the fire, silent and dazed as Jordan and Devin rejoined us and sat down.

"That bugger almost got me at the top of the run," Devin said. "After that big hole on the left, the current goes directly toward the big wall of water. I had to fight like hell to keep out of it."

"It looked six or seven feet high from where we stood.

What do you think?" Jordan asked.

"That seems about right," Devin said. "The raft would have been chewed up like a dishrag, and I'd be sharing the splints with Kyle. Three-foot-diameter boulders are churning around in that mess. I can't believe Kyle is still breathing."

"How can water lift a rock weighing hundreds of pounds?" I asked. "Okay, it could roll them along the bottom, but lift them to the top?"

"It doesn't seem rational, I admit, but it's really a simple thing," Devin answered. "The fast water picks up sand and silt, which is suspended, and the sheer mass of that concoction is heavier than the big rocks. All the deep canyons were carved out by these flash floods hurling rocks into the side walls. That was all before we started controlling the flooding. Actually, it was before humans walked the planet."

"But still," I said, "that's a lot of carving for a few rocks."

Devin nodded. "A few million years and it gets the job done. Things take time."

"Did you get a look at that snake?" I asked.

"Rattler. Poisonous. Good thing you killed it," Devin said softly.

"Well, I thought Jordan was going to teach it the polka. I mean, she was fearless with that monster," I said.

Devin looked over at Jordan and said, "You're a city girl with a lot of guts, that's for sure."

We sat around the fire, finishing the hot chili. The previous nights' arrogant boasting, political arguments and sharp-witted frivolity were all absent. Pat sipped a beer. A bottle of Jack Daniels, from some unknown source, slowly passed around the group. The three bright stars of Orion's belt stared at me once again, but this time through a clear, blue sky. I had no inspiring insights, and I gazed up with thoughts only of tomorrow and getting off this river. The group thinned out, and Pat and I sat alone in silence around the smoldering blaze for a while. Time for sleep, I thought. I got up without a word and headed back to my tent.

When I got there, the front door flaps were flung to the sides, so I stooped forward, ducked my head, and started to shimmy into the small, narrow enclosure. A flashlight suddenly illuminated my feet, and I looked up, a little startled.

"Don't get the wrong idea," said Jordan. "I'm just in here for snake protection. You killed the first one. I'm counting on you for defense."

I stood kneeling, frozen for a few seconds. Neither one of us said a word. Then I lifted my right hand and reached forward. I cupped Jordan's soft cheek in my palm and gently kissed her mouth. Her lips were soft and wet, melting like warm honey against mine. Her arms opened and pulled me into the tent next to her. She lifted her head and kissed me, then rolled onto her back, dragging me on top, while her hand rested on the small of my back and pressed my body against hers. The small flashlight slipped under the sleeping bag, and the tent was dark except for a glimmer of moonlight seeping through the thin nylon walls.

18

A young boy stood at home plate, staring at the infield of a sun-roasted baseball diamond in Murfreesboro, Tennessee. As the pitcher's foot pawed the mound and he contemplated the next pitch, the game's slow pace unnerved the young batter. His feet would not stand still, his eyes darted, and his whole body vibrated with the expectation of the next pitch.

He was capable of swinging the bat and making solid connection with the ball, but patience to wait for a hittable ball, eluded the young player. The first pitch came flying across the plate, and the boy twisted his waist and shoulders forward. Arms and bat followed with a ferocious cut through the thick, humid, Southern air.

High and outside—should have let it go, waited for a better one, taken a breath, stepped out of the batter's box.

Control the pace of the game. I knew what to do, but I couldn't tell him. I wanted him to look at me, but he kept staring at the pitcher and the infield.

Suddenly he stepped out of the box and looked at the left- field bleachers and gave a quick wave with his right hand. Fourth-row center, waving back, was a forty-ish, slim man with a receding hairline and dressed in business slacks and a white shirt. He wore aviator sunglasses but no hat. It was his dad, I was sure. I tried to get a better look but couldn't see. The man looked familiar to me.

"I was hitting well in practice this week. Coach says I need to settle in," the boy said, as if talking directly to the fourth- row bleachers.

"Just wait for a good one and watch the ball leave the pitcher's hand," his dad said from the bleachers in a quiet, confident voice. "Keep your eye on that ball. You'll hit it."

I glanced back at home plate. The boy was still looking deep in the outfield. Then he stroked the dirt with his left foot and glared down the third-base line. The next pitch found the center of his white hickory bat. The third baseman extended his glove and leaped into the air, but the ball soared into left field, farther and farther, until it disappeared in a murky haze.

My eyes opened slowly, and I focused on the top of the moon drenched tent only two feet above. I felt like rubbing my eyes, but didn't want to expend the effort to pull my arms out of the warm bag. Jordan was beside me facing the tent wall. She had a small stocking cap on her head, covering the only part of her body not deep in the sleeping bag. I bent sideways and looked out of the open tent door. The fire was smoldering, the air was calm, the camp totally quiet. After zipping up the tent flap, I buried myself back in the bag next to Jordan and once more fell asleep.

19

The early-morning light faintly filled the tent as I began to focus, opening one sleepy eye at a time.

"Hey there, snake killer," Jordan whispered in my ear.

I turned to see her brown eyes wide open and staring at me. She didn't wear makeup and didn't need it. The glow from her rosy cheeks was back, and the gleam in her eyes gave her a natural beauty. She had an inner attractiveness that transcended the physical, a deeply confident character. But even the toughest people can go over the cliff, and yesterday Jordan was definitely edging past her limits. Today she sounded like her old self. Everybody's vulnerable sometime, I thought.

Anyway, this romance thing was going a little fast for even me. A fearless titan of business, here I was helpless in the clutches of love.

"You're quite a chick," I said softly.

"Just what I needed early in the morning," she said. "A derogatory term that equates me to a small, defenseless animal."

I made no reply and waited to see how much trouble I was in. She shoved the palm of her hand against my shoulder and rolled me over on my back. Before I could resist, she crawled over and slammed her lips on mine in a hard, fierce kiss. Both of her hands darted to the sides of my rib cage, and she began tickling. I rolled from side to side, trying to break her grip. She kept her mouth plastered to mine, muffling my giddy laughter. Finally, I broke loose.

"Okay, okay, you're not a chick," I blurted.

"I like being a chick. It means you have to do everything for me. I'm helpless and need waiting on. Let's get started. Peel me a grape."

"You're not a chick. I give up."

"This must mean you're a 'cool dude,'" she said. "Let's see, what do you need to be the coolest? A mustang convertible, or maybe a yellow and black Mini Cooper— drop-top, of course. A spike haircut—yeah, get rid of that frumpy look. You need some of those pants that hang around your hips to make sure your boxer shorts can be seen by the general public. I've got it: for more formal occasions, you need those four-hundred-dollar blue jeans that are ripped up and shredded. I'm giving you a real makeover, mister."

She wore a huge grin and was reveling like a little girl in this fantasy. I rose up on my elbow and stopped her banter with a gentle kiss, my left hand tenderly caressing the tickle-center of her rib cage.

She pulled away and whispered, "Don't you dare."

Without a word, my hand rotated inward to stroke her bare breast.

"That's better," she said.

20

The rocks were covered with a light layer of morning dew, and even the usually dry summer moss had a soft, rain- soaked look. The guides moved like a precision machine, packing the raft. A five-foot slab of plywood that had been the platform for strapping sleeping bags and kitchen gear was tied securely across the backend of the raft. A tree had been selected about fifty yards from the riverbank, and the large food coolers, tents, and other gear were being piled next to it to be picked up later.

"Bag your tent and sleeping gear, Casanova, and put it next to the tree," Devin shouted while looking straight at me. "A boat will float down next week to pick it all up."

"Okay. What can I help with?" I asked.

"Put some padding on that slab of plywood. We're going to strap Kyle down to get through Gunslinger rapid. The helicopter pickup is just beyond it at Horseshoe Camp. The Forest Service cleared a helipad after the big fire. The rapid is a class two, but it'll run fast today."

"How is he?" I asked.

"The shoulder is about the same, but the knee is turning black and his stomach is swelling. There's coffee and some bread and jelly. That's it for breakfast." Devin then walked briskly toward the boats.

Jordan was crouched next to Kyle when I stuck my head into his tent.

"You holding in there, buddy?" I asked, knowing the answer was not a good one.

"I'll be whipping Jordan around the dance floor tonight, no problem," Kyle said with a quiet whisper.

"Yeah you will. We're putting you in first class for the remainder of the flight, buddy. Hold your own."

I backed slowly out of the small entrance and stood quietly alone next to the tent under an old white pine tree. I looked up to see stripped lower branches, remnants of old limbs broken at the ends still holding on to the massive trunk, useless and weary but still part of the proud tree. No breeze rustled through the evergreen canopy. The dead air was only a blank canvas for the droning sound of the river. I could hear the muffled voices of Jordan and Kyle, and then, as if on stage delivering a lecture, Kyle started talking in a clear, distinct voice.

"You need to know about the book," he began.

"Just take it easy, now," Jordan broke in. "You can tell me all about it when you're stronger."

"No, listen, I want you to hear this," he insisted. "I didn't ever want to write a book for a group of tree huggers. Most of what's in there is questionable science made up by...well, I don't know who wrote that stuff."

"Wait," Jordan said. "You mean, you didn't write it?"
"No. I didn't know much about global warming at the time. The publisher called me from New York and asked if I would be a part of this book they were putting together that coincided with my research about global temperature variations. They would provide most of the material through a ghostwriter, but they wanted me to write a chapter on species' reaction to climate change. I had no work on that, but they offered a five-thousand-dollar advance for the entire piece, so I dummied up a chapter on it, thinking they would add it to the research work that they wanted to publish."

"Dummied it up?" Jordan replied.

"I had heard a little about it, so I wrote up what I knew, like I was an expert. No big deal, I did it a thousand times in college. Everybody does."

"Kyle, I can't believe you are telling me this," Jordan said. "That book was massive, and it made you millions of dollars."

"Exactly," he continued in almost a whisper. "When the book came out, I was in shock. It was a bestseller immediately. I got calls for interviews and TV appearances, but I didn't know anything about the book that actually came out, or this whole subject of warming. So, I rooted around and found a lawyer—I'd never needed a lawyer before—to stop that book from being distributed with my name on it. He got nowhere for a couple of months, and then a six-hundred-thousand-dollar check arrived. It was an advance royalty payment. I'd never seen that much money before. Anyway, the ball was rolling, and I couldn't stop it."

"This is blowing my mind," Jordan said after a brief silence. "I didn't think things like that happened. That book was fake? Is that what I'm hearing?"

"It was real, all right. It's just I didn't write it, and I couldn't verify the science of this whole global warming theory. There is a fine line between dealing with facts and making a point. What I mean is that if all these facts, which are inconclusive, are interpreted one way, it's not seen as urgent, and nobody cares. If they are looked at a different way, the argument takes on a more compelling tone."

"You mean the science behind this isn't real?"

"It's data, but unverified and not replicated by any other scientists, and the interpretation of it is skewed so the man-made global warming argument would be compelling."

"What about all this carbon emission rhetoric?" Jordan asked.

"It looks like carbon dioxide is building in the atmosphere, but the man-made portion may be only around one percent of the increase. Higher levels of carbon are natural in a warming planet like we've had for the last ten thousand years. But the rub here is that carbon dioxide is a poor greenhouse gas. Water vapor accounts for ninety-five percent of the greenhouse effect. Carbon dioxide is not much of a factor, at least not much that anybody can prove."

There was a pause from Kyle, and it seemed Jordan couldn't muster a reply. Then, in a low voice, Kyle continued.

"Carbon is less than four-tenths of a percent of the

atmosphere. It's fairly inconsequential. Anyway, weather changes all the time in areas, including the polar regions, but the primary determinant to actual global climate change is the orbital variations of the earth and sun."

"I'm not sure I follow you," Jordan said.

"Our existence on this planet is dependent on the sun. Without it, this would be a frozen ball of rock. The earth rotates on an angle, and that angle changes a few degrees over long periods of time, putting some areas closer and some further away from the light source." Kyle stopped and took a long breath. "That's the primary source of climate change."

"Where are all the carbon dioxide increases coming from?" Jordan asked.

"There are a lot of possible sources," Kyle continued. "Undersea volcanic eruptions can produce huge amounts of carbon dioxide that no scientist can measure. There is no complete picture."

"So what did you do about the book?" Jordan asked. "What could I do? I practically memorized the whole book, did the interviews, and went on TV. My career skyrocketed, and I made a ton of money."

There was a long pause; the wind still lay calm, and only the river gave its reply. Kyle was talking through the codeine, babbling on, I thought. Nobody was saying it, but we all knew that he might not make it. Was this his last confession?

"Whether the science is right or not, there is a huge benefit to this entire campaign," Kyle spoke, breaking the quiet, his raspy, strained voice trailing off after each sentence. "And this is what I feel good about. We are able to hold polluters accountable and clean up the environment. There is a momentum toward sustainable energy, today, that would never have happened without our movement."

"Sustainable is good, Kyle," Jordan said in a slightly patronizing way.

But, lying? I thought to myself.

"If the global warming theory is right, we could see huge changes that will affect agriculture, snow, and rainfall. Whole populations could be wiped out. But, the feedback loops might work in our favor and dissipate this pollution faster than we think. The truth is, nobody really knows." He paused and there was silence. "The pollution cleanup is the hidden agenda of global warming, and has got to be done, and everybody needs to help, Jordan."

Devin's voice echoed through the campsite with instructions. Then Jordan opened the flap and emerged from the tent. She looked up at me, startled, and not expecting to see me, but her expression acknowledged that I had heard the whole thing.

"Wow," I said under my breath.

Jordan nestled her cheek onto my chest and laid her head on my shoulder.

"How far to the pickup?" she asked, with a sad resolve in her voice.

"About half a mile to the camp and another mile to the vans, one rapid left to run."

"He can't take much jostling. He's bad, really bad," she replied. "I guess it was his confession. He's a sweet guy."

We both felt like talking about this astonishing revelation, just as a way of trying to understand what it meant to us, and really, the whole world, but there was no time, and this was not the place.

21

When I got to the riverbank, Pat was in his kayak, executing turns in a patch of still water. He looked up and nodded but said nothing. He was dealing with the stress in his own way. Simon stood silently on the bank, facing downriver. He turned toward me. His right arm rose slowly, till his hand touched the bill of his Los Angeles Dodgers hat in a "Good morning" gesture.

"You kayaking today?" I asked, not thinking it was a good idea this soon after his injury.

"I'm feeling better today," said Simon, with firm resolve. "No dizziness. The swelling is down. They have their hands full with Kyle. I can handle it."

"After we meet the helicopter, we have about a mile

stretch before the takeout," I said, trying to sound positive. "I've been through tougher stuff than this."

He paused, settled back on his heels and took a long, deep breath.

"When I was a kid, I lived in Iran. The Shah was running things then. There was some favoritism, and the rich got richer, but there was order. And more importantly, you could get an education and a career if you worked hard."

He paused again, and seemed to be waiting for the words to formulate in his mind.

"Then the religious fanatics moved in. That was when the American embassy was stormed and taken over. You probably remember that. The whole thing took place in about four-square blocks in Tehran." Simon ambled around the small beach as he talked.

"Watching it on TV, it looked like the whole country was coming apart," I said softly.

"That's television for you. They fill a twenty-seven-inch screen with four blocks of chaos. But anyway, the country started to change radically after that. The clerics took over the government, and policies and religion restricted freedom of speech, trade, and education. The bottom dropped out of the economy, and if it weren't for oil revenue, things would have been really bad. Never planned to go back, but I made a few unplanned trips."

"Why did you go back?" I asked.

Simon paused, shuffled his feet in an uncomfortable little dance, and said, "Let's just say I had to take care of some family business."

My mind churned with a plethora of questions, but I kept quiet. What was this deep, dark secret that Simon was hiding? What kind of surreptitious past did this good- natured physician have?

Finally, he turned halfway toward me in an accommodating gesture and spoke in a low, gentle voice. I felt like some truths were going to be revealed.

"The best moment of my life was a dance I had in Seattle in 1979," he said. "A waltz. I was at a ballroom dancing class—a little shy and a little lonely.

"For some reason," he continued, "they were playing a very schmaltzy version of 'The Tennessee Waltz.' It was an old ballroom—worn-out paint, creaky floors, those wooden chairs with padded, blue cushions with about half of them loosing their stuffing. A bright green spotlight was mounted on the wall shining on a rotating glass ball that reflected tiny specks of light everywhere. I had been eyeing this very beautiful girl and finally got up the courage to walk across the room to ask her to dance. When she looked up, her green eyes seemed to open like windows to a new world. Her light brown hair broke on top of her shoulders, and her cream complexion glowed even in that dark room. But what made it the best was the way she glided in my arms across the floor, effortless with every step. She was a much better dancer than me, but made me feel like Fred Astaire. We danced the whole song, and on the last note I pulled my hand up from her waist to the middle of her back, shifted my weight to my left foot, and dipped her backward. She took my cue like a ballerina, arched her back, and dropped her head below her shoulders, making a gentle curve from the tip of her toe to the top of her head."

I muttered something like "Cool" but felt anything I could say would fall short of the moment. He stood lost in his faraway time, and then, as if the music mysteriously came echoing through the trees, he was dancing with the beautiful girl from Seattle. His right arm was in front of him, leveled at shoulder height, his left around her waist. He two-stepped around the beach, and I think he heard nothing but "The Tennessee Waltz."

Devin and Pat stood on the deck of the raft, watching the would-be ballroom in the sand. After a few more dance moves, Simon twisted and, in a single motion, bent his knees, picked up a handful of paddles, and stepped toward the raft. I kept my eyes straight ahead, hoping to mask my utter bewilderment. Then I dropped my chin, turned, pointed my shoulders toward the bank, and walked out of that ballroom forever.

22

The plywood was lashed tightly to the back of the raft. On top, a stack of sleeping mats cushioned the ride. Devin had fastened packing straps to the raft's metal frame, and they were tightened securely over Kyle and his red life jacket. Then the raft pushed off into the deep, slow- running pool in front of the campsite. Devin sat in the center perch, fully in control of the craft, both hands on the oars while the younger guide that usually ran the raft sat in the back with Kyle. Our kayaks followed and, after about five hundred yards, I heard the roar of the rapid.

"Run it down the right side through those small waves," said Pat, "and as soon as you hit the first big one, point your bow left and paddle hard across the river. The current runs into a big rock and you want to miss it—the rock, that is. Devin is not sure how it will actually run in this high water, but past that rock there shouldn't be any obstacles, just a lot of fast water. Eddy out on the right downstream and let's regroup."

Simon hit the first waves and cut through them with speed and momentum. His paddle dug into the gurgling flow on the left and pushed forward slightly causing his boat to lurch, and he hit the next wave head-on with the big rock safely off his right gunnel.

The current pulled Jordan into the first wave a little cockeyed, which threw the nose of her boat to the right. She stuck her paddle deep into the water and executed a firm back stroke. The nose jutted left but the wave washed her into the big rock. She executed a hard-forward stroke, leaned her body into the rock while the water lifted her up and slammed her into the four-foot hole below. With her next stroke, the wave collapsed over her bow, but she easily punched through to the quiet water below.

I hit the first waves with determination and confidence. As I descended toward the big roller, a series of small ripples tossed my bow sideways, throwing me out of control into the wave and toward the rock. The rush of water lifted my boat onto the polished granite. Then, like yesterday, I made the fatal mistake. I leaned away from the rock and the boat rolled, exposing the inside cavity to the rushing current. I slipped out of the boat like a limp doll in a windstorm, heading straight to the bottom. The current pushed me and I popped to the surface about ten feet downstream.

Grabbing the side of Pat's boat, I pulled myself across his bow and just laid there, catching my breath and waiting for the raft to shoot the rapid.

My confidence shaken and my lungs still gasping for air, I heard Pat say in a low, quiet voice, "Good place for trout. Got everything they need right here, just need four things and it's Mecca-city for fish."

Pat was small talking to calm me down, and probably himself too. Nobody could be interested in fishing in a swollen, flooded river with injuries and uncertainties and Kyle about to die—not even Pat, I thought.

Just then Simon floated my kayak over, and I climbed into the river-drenched seat as we watched the raft enter the fast water. Devin steered the left pontoon into the first waves and the boat rocked gently side to side. A simultaneous back stroke on the left and a hard-forward paddle on the right swung the front of the boat around, pointing across the river. A couple of power strokes thrust the raft into the big wave, and it skipped over the water to the top of the curl and stopped all forward motion, just surfing the wave. On the boat, Devin looked confident and calm, but a glance over at Jordan offered a different story.

She had stopped all motion, her eyes fixed on the raft. Eventually it slid off the center and into the big rock. Devin reacted quickly with a hard-back stroke, causing the pontoon to bounce off the rock surface and rotate into the lower curl with a half turn. The stern collapsed into the hole sideways but straightened when it hit the wave thanks to another quick paddle stroke. The raft floated in next to us, and Devin checked on Kyle, whose wide eyes mirrored his helpless, hysterical fear.

Ten minutes later, we pulled into the Horseshoe campground, which spread out a thousand yards into a flat, wide canyon that was a patch of sand and small brush. We lined the kayaks up on the beach and moved Kyle onto the sand. Jordan rushed over but found him barely able to focus, his eyes opening only occasionally.

"They better get here quick or we're gong to lose him," she whispered.

"I called in to the airport right after we cleared Gunslinger. They're in the air now. You guys pull the raft under that tree and cinch it up. When the chopper touches down, the rotors will airlift these boats." Devin sounded like the captain of the *USS Whatever*.

"So these kayaks are goners?" I asked, wishing I had kept my mouth shut.

"The kayaks, with you guys in them, will be floating down the river when that bird lands," Devin continued. "Get everything you need and get ready to push off. Pick a spot and wait for me downstream. The vans will meet us at a takeout spot in about a mile. Not as fancy as the one I promised yesterday, but it'll do."

We found a quiet stretch to wait downstream and could hear the rotary blades of the helicopter cutting through the moist morning air. The branches bent and flexed in a wild flurry of hysterical motion as the chopper disappeared from our line of sight under the tree line, touching down on the littered sand beach.

In no more than five minutes, the air began churning again, and the helicopter rose above us in near vertical flight. I kept my eyes glued to the horizon as it flew up and out, transforming into a small dot and disappearing over the canyon rim.

23

The sun was low when we finished loading the vans and started up the narrow, winding, one-lane road to the highway above. In two hours, we pulled into a motel in McCall. Dressed up twenty-somethings strolled into the jazz club next door, and a new strip mall marquis advertised the usual discount stores across the street. Civilization never looked so uncivilized to me, I thought, while I helped unload the duffels. Jordan walked out of the lobby and handed each one of us a magnetic card key. "Gentlemen, your rooms are ready," she said with a sheepish grin.

Simon reached out through obvious exhaustion, hugged her, and gave her a fatherly kiss on the cheek. No words needed to be spoken, as each worn-out river rat grabbed his bag and disappeared through the lobby. I threw my duffel on my shoulder and headed for room 382.

Dropping my bag into an empty elevator, the third-floor button lit up as I gave it a sharp stab. I don't even have her phone number, I thought. What difference does it make? A fling is a fling. Los Angeles is full of more exciting men than me. I'm almost old enough to be her father. Anyway, the kids would kill me if I hooked up with Jordan. Too young.

The card key glided into the narrow slit, a green dot flashed on the handle, and the door opened quietly. I tossed my bag next to the closet and looked up to see a bottle of champagne in a small, green plastic ice bucket on the credenza. Pretty nice for an Econo hotel, I thought to myself.

"Thought you'd never show up," I heard her say. Propped up with two pillows on the bed in TV-watching position, Jordan sat in camp shorts and a T-shirt. I walked over and sat on the bed next to her.

"Devin just called," she said. "It's about Kyle."

I felt the blood rush from my head to my feet along with a sharp, low jab in my temples.

"He made it to the hospital in McCall, and they're moving him to Boise tomorrow. He's going to make it."

"Thank God," I said as I dropped my chin and closed my eyes.

Neither one of us said a word. The silence said everything. I kicked my shoes off, reached for the champagne and brought two glasses over and sat next to the bed stand.

Looking directly into her eyes, I took her hand in mine and said, "Lillykile beer?"

"Yeah, well, my dad was the creative type," she said with a slight wink.

"Did all his stories have morbid moral lessons?" I asked.

"He was a rugged individualist. What can I say? He was my dad," she said in nearly a whisper.

Then I leaned down and kissed her hand politely like you would the hand of a queen. I kissed her wrist and gently moved to the soft skin inside her forearm. Opening my mouth, I let my teeth softly bear down upon her arm as if biting her, then grunted playfully. My left hand darted to her rib cage, and my fingers dug tenderly into the soft, ticklish skin. She started to roll her body and thrash at the same time. Like a flash, her hands found the soft, underarm flesh covering my ribs.

"You're dead meat, mister!" she shouted.

I rolled over, trying to pull away from her devilish

tickle, but she rolled on top of me and then suddenly stopped. I lifted my head off the pillow and kissed her. The shopping center lights peeked through a crack in the drawn curtains, and there was a faint hint of jazz from below.

Just enough civilization, I thought.

THE END

ABOUT THE AUTHOR

Along with *The Purple River*, Best Selling Author, Rick Glaze, published *Eight Pieces of Eight* in 2025 and *Spanish Pieces of Eight*, a sailing adventure/mystery in 2022, *Jackass a Short Story Collection* in 2022, and *Ralph & Murray* in 2024. Rick was a financial columnist in Silicon Valley for San Francisco's *Nob Hill Gazette* and the *Los Altos Town Crier*. He attended the Stanford University Creative Writing Program, and is a graduate of Peabody College, Vanderbilt University. An award-winning songwriter, with a Pandora station and Spotify Playlist, credits on Country Music Television (CMT), and BBC Radio, Rick has rafted the Grand Canyon, the Salmon and Rogue Rivers as well as sailed throughout the Caribbean Sea.